QUESTION NOT MY SALT

Amanda M. Blake

Crystal Lake Entertainment
www.CrystalLakePub.com

"Deliciously macabre and astoundingly fresh, *Question Not My Salt* is a richly prepared buffet of weirdness and depravity. Blake has crafted a truly grim offering about tradition that will disturb and shock even the most discriminating connoisseurs of body horror."

— Eric LaRocca, author of
Things Have Gotten Worse Since We Last Spoke

"Blake invites us to a feast so tantalizing you won't be able to look away, even as your stomach does flips. It's as delicious as it is depraved. Bon appetit."

— Lor Gislason, author of *Inside Out*

My mom always told me to never go to someone's home empty-handed. She did not elaborate on what constituted full hands. I don't know their dietary restrictions anyway, and I'm too young to buy wine. I consider bringing a multi-pack of soft tissue. It's cold and flu season after all. That's considerate, right?

But when I asked my roommate whether that would be a good gift to bring, she looked at me like I had a mouthful of lizards. Then she laughed and told me to bring grocery store sugar cookies, because I can't hope to compare with Mother's cooking.

That's what she calls her parents: Mother and Father. I hear the capitalization, and with it, reverence that I'm not used to, since I sometimes call my mom Mom, other times Melanie, other times Goober. The way Zoe refers to them feels old-fashioned, but I like it. After listening to her long enough, they're Mother and Father to me, too.

I brought grocery store sugar cookies decorated with autumn-colored sprinkles, plus a bottle of sparkling grape juice for people like me who feel uncomfortable around wine glasses. Not because of my own problems or anything. My parents had me try wine, beer, vodka, and rum in the controlled environment of our home. I only liked the rum, but I prefer ginger ale. I've never been in a hurry to sprint to the spirit aisle—not least because my Aunt Lila and Uncle Farnon's wine and bourbon bottles contribute half the recycled glass of their commonwealth. They always bring their own clinking crate to holiday gatherings.

But this year, I don't have to field Uncle Farnon's drunken dirty jokes or Aunt Lila's oversharing by the time they reach the end of their respective bottles, nor my cousin Eddy nicking

Corona Lights all night and thinking we can't smell it on his breath, or my cousin Gigi with their skunk-sweet pot on the back porch. Not even Aunt Jeanette's pecan pie can make up for the deterioration of inhibitions and patience by the end of a family holiday feast.

This year, I'm not going home for Thanksgiving. Not only is it not worth the hectic flight, but Canadian Thanksgiving is in October—which I also missed, because it's not an American holiday and we didn't get days off for it.

So when Zoe invited me to join her family for my first American Thanksgiving, I jumped at the opportunity.

"We always invite friends," she said. "They're like adopted family. You won't be out of place at all, and I think you'll have a really good time."

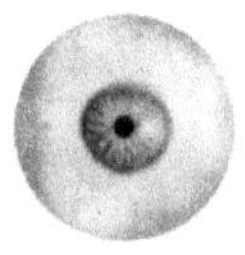

I'm nervous in the driveway and sick by the front porch, a concrete slab with a welcome mat that literally says *Welcome*. The front door is festooned with a giant wreath nest for the tumbleweed-and-feather turkey sitting in its swing with a sign that reads *Eat Well, Give Thanks*.

The stars and stripes and a Dallas Cowboys flag flutter behind me in the unseasonably frigid breeze. Unseasonable for them, not for me. Oh, I get cold like everyone else, but there's something to knowing how to dress for it, even if you never quite get used to it. And that goes for the sweltering San

Antonio heat down here most months out of the year, which I was not prepared for at all.

Zoe's shivering, and I'm not, but I still want to go into a warm house, even if I have no idea what to expect on the inside of this one. I moved so far away from my home to try something new, be around people I'd never have met otherwise, surround myself with unfamiliar architecture, flora, fauna. That's what college is for, right? Broadening minds with new experiences? But wanting is different than having. Zoe knows better than anyone that I've barely left the dorm for anything other than classes or food. Because I didn't know anyone going in, it's not the easiest thing for me to make friends. Plenty of friendly people, sure, and I do try to be friendly back, but I don't plan to pledge, and at bake sales, you can only talk about chocolate so many ways.

As they say down here, Zoe's been a blessing, especially since she doesn't go to church on Sundays, either. It seems like everyone else around us does so religiously—pun intended—or sleeps in as a form of rebellion against being forced to do so the rest of the time. I was raised in an agnostic household that celebrated holidays for the gifts and the booze. Zoe looks down on what she calls shallow-faithed Bible-thumpers watching their weekly religious show rather than living their truth. I don't know what that means, but she didn't hang any crosses in our room, doesn't say grace out loud when we eat together in the dorm, hasn't sacrificed a mourning dove on an ersatz altar in our closet, and she makes snickerdoodles in the communal kitchen every Saturday and offers me half, so I figure we're good.

I bring cookies and cider, but Zoe's not a guest; she brings her bright, sparkling smile when she opens the front door and Mother is there to greet her with generous open arms.

"Oh, sweetie, it's so good to see you again. It's been way too long! I thought the reason you went to school so close was so you could come home more often. Look at you. You need a good meal in you. What have they been feeding you?"

"Nothing as good as what you make." Zoe hugs Mother with just as much enthusiasm, as though it's been four years instead of four months, although I don't remember Zoe ever saying anything about missing home. "And you just saw me last week."

Mother fake-spits to the side. "Video chat isn't the same. I can't hug you through a screen, even though I hug the computer afterward. Don't I hug the computer afterward, George?"

"She does. Every time the screen goes dark, she closes the laptop and hugs it to her chest. She says she hopes you feel it through the Internet." Like Mother, Father is all smiles and sun-spotted skin. They are warm in their crow's feet and crackling-hearth voices.

"Mother, you're embarrassing me. This is Sierra, my roommate." Zoe brings me forward to be engulfed in a stranger's arms, and honestly, I'm not mad. My family isn't very touchy-feely, so it's uncomfortable, yet somehow as comfortable as Zoe's snickerdoodles. I don't know what to do with my hands, but Mother smells like pumpkin spices. I need my pumpkin spice latte from September through December. I inhale her like milk foam.

"Happy Thanksgiving, Sierra, and thank you so much for helping take care of my baby girl," Mother murmurs into my hair.

"She takes care of me more," I say back.

The hug lasts longer than I expect from a stranger. I don't know if I'm allowed to pull back or if she's the one who decides. I release when she releases.

"Now, as I understand it, this is your first Thanksgiving?"

"Well, I've had lots of Thanksgivings, but not American. Ours can be similar, but it's not the same. It's not quite…*this.*" I gesture to nothing in particular, but the burning three-wick candles, fake fall leaves, and themed throw pillows and blankets all around the foyer seem to answer my vagaries.

"Oh, you're in for a treat. We celebrate all holidays like it's our last, but we love Thanksgiving the most."

Her arm around my shoulder, Mother leads me deeper into the house. It's darker than I expect, with more walls than fashionable and heavy drapes half-closed on the windows rather than letting in natural light. The décor is cozy—dark walls in warm colors, sitting furniture upholstered in cool colors, furniture and paneling in stained wood, golden and russet hues all the way to black. A set of stairs lead up to the second floor, but Mother walks me past that, away from the parlor and study on either side of the foyer.

The back of the house opens wide into a cavern of loudly conversing family. Two massive live-edge tables end to end straddle the dining room and part of the family room across from the kitchen, where rolling butcher-block islands expand the counter space.

While the front of the house smelled like cinnamon and sandalwood, the back smells like Mother: pumpkin spices, turkey stuffing, sautéing mushrooms and sausage, candied carrots, toasted pecans, fresh bread. There are bowls of ingredients, covered pots and pans, wooden spoons dripping with sauce and gravy, and three chef ovens set to different temperatures and times.

People are everywhere—milling on stools around the kitchen, slouching on the dining room benches and window seat, lounging on the large sectional and assortment of armchairs and ottomans in the sunken family room. The fireplace burns like a heart, and the huge plasma screen is set to mute on the National Dog Show. Everyone ramps up their volume to be heard over everyone else's conversations, so both smell and sound assault me all at once.

"Don't worry about being the only one here who isn't family," Mother says, upping her volume as well, although it seems more effortless for her. When she speaks, the rest of the family modulates softer. "All of us make a point to invite people who might not be able to go home or don't have a home to go to. It's not like we don't have enough food. Desserts on that island, dear, and drinks with the wine and soda bottles."

Mother points me to the island of desserts near the bay window, which has other grocery-bought items with plastic packaging and printed ingredient lists as well as humbler baked goods like pumpkin bread, pecan tassies, and Mexican wedding cookies. On the sideboard next to the dessert island, glass bottles of wine and plastic bottles of soda—some opened, others waiting—stand awkwardly among buckets of ice melting in the crowd-warmed air. My cider and cookies get lost, but I don't think anyone will miss them.

"Have you had anything to eat today yet?"

"No, ma'am." She seems like someone I'm supposed to say 'ma'am' to. "I didn't know how much food there'd be."

Mother laughs. "Oh, enough food for three days, but we don't start eating for another four hours. I don't normally allow appetizers, but get yourself some pumpkin bread and soda so your belly doesn't grumble for too long. Oh, Sierra, Zoe didn't tell me if you have any dietary restrictions."

I shake my head. I have preferences, but no restrictions.

"Good, because we have a little of everything around here. Flour, salt, lard, meat… That's how I make it, so that's how it is."

Mother leads me back into the kitchen so that she can tend to her pots. She's the only one working on the meal. My grandma prods the back of my mind, telling me to ask if I can help in any way, but the huge dining room table is already set, and I can barely make powdered mashed potatoes. A woman whose mission is to make a Thanksgiving feast on her own for over three dozen people would waste time trying to teach me how to do whatever needs to be done. So I follow another piece of grandmotherly wisdom: I keep my hands behind my back and my mouth shut.

Zoe follows Father into the family room, where she greets siblings and cousins, aunts and uncles. She seems to know everybody, even the ones who appear just as out of place as I do. I envy her ease.

Mother gestures for one of her nieces, nephews, or in-laws

to pass over a stool for me. I perch next to her to watch her witchery while I eat chocolate chip pumpkin bread, which is homemade and good. I bet she can make better, though.

"Did Zoe tell you how Thanksgiving works around here?" Mother asks. She speaks softly now, just the two of us in her kitchen, with the bubble and steam of her fragrant pots and pans cancelling out the rest of the room. If there were a cat tangling between my feet, I think I'd be in heaven.

"I didn't know there's an itinerary, no."

Mother laughs with her whole body, a ripple through her flesh, without shame or concern about being too loud or showing too much of the inside of her mouth. "I prep, clean, and cook for a week before the feast. You better believe we have an itinerary. We cut guests slack, because even if you've had a Thanksgiving feast of your very own, it's not enough to prepare you for what the Samuels family has in store. I just want you to know some of what you can expect for the rest of the day. Are you a morning bird or a night owl?"

"I'm a college student. College students are obligate owls."

"We're traditionalists at heart, my family. We love Thanksgiving and go all out, which means our celebrations last longer than other families'. The feast is a marathon, not a sprint. No computers, no phones, no television, no Christmas music—not until Thanksgiving is done. We put up the tree tomorrow with Nat King Cole and Bing Crosby and the Carpenters, but we prefer to appreciate the holiday we're in."

Mother tastes the gravy, then turns the heat down to a simmer.

"Like I said, there are no appetizers, nothing to spoil your appetite—except wine, but we only drink in moderation here. I know we're not going to have any trouble like that from you."

If she had glasses, she would look over them at me in anticipation of disapproval, but I emphatically shake my head.

"We've had things get out of hand around here before. If that happens, we take them to the quiet room to put themselves together. I don't mind a little libation to lubricate conversation, but the point of the feast is to enjoy it, not forget about it in a blackout. And drunk people are only entertaining to other drunk people."

A-fucking-men. Which I don't say aloud. I don't know Mother's position on swear words, but I'm sure it's impolite when we've only just met.

"We rarely do that anymore. By now, the family knows better. It's really the ones who marry in who have to learn. They learn quickly, though."

Mother beckons for another rolling island, which is already set with unpeeled carrots. Her family hops to, bending over backward to give her what she needs right when she needs it. She uses a peeler with a confident speed. I'd peel the skin off my own finger if I tried to mimic her.

"We start our meal at two. Everyone sits at the table. We say grace. Then we have courses all the way to midnight. Instead of stuffing our faces for an hour before watching the game, we record the game and save it for after the festivities so we can take the time to enjoy every bit of the feast in parts rather than one bloated whole. Ten hours of a feast may sound like a lot, but we do other things between courses that work up an appetite. We play games. We laugh. We cry. We don't get full, and no one ever goes hungry. Do you have anywhere you need to be before midnight?"

"No." Everything I need to get done during the holiday, I scheduled for the weekend. However, I can't imagine doing nothing but eating for ten whole hours, even with games interspersed between the servings. Sometimes I *dream* about doing nothing but eating for ten whole hours, but that's calorie-free and unrealistic. Even if I were to slow down the ritual of eating to focus on each piece, each bite, boredom eventually creeps in.

Doubt must show in my expression, although I try to conceal my feelings like a good guest.

"Oh, don't worry, dear, it's not the chore it sounds like. We promise good food and good company, a true testament to giving thanks for our blessings and sharing some of those blessings with others. You won't even know it's midnight by the time we wind down."

"Is that why you close the curtains?" Despite the late morning, the cave-like quality of the room makes it feel like seven at night.

"We Samuelses are just a little sensitive to light." She prods at the dark circles under her eyes, from genetics rather than weariness. Above the shallow capillaries, the pale blue of her irises glints uncannily in the kitchen light.

I nod. Zoe keeps the dorm room dark, blinds drawn and closed all day, and only a lamp or two on. She has prescription transition lenses that are specially made to stay dark even inside. She only takes them off in the dorm room. I don't mind, but when I know she's going to be out, I open the blinds and soak up vitamin D until she returns.

"In our own homes, we tend to keep things shadowed. Are you having trouble seeing?"

"No, I can see fine." I fear I've asked something wrong, but Mother doesn't appear angry.

"Good. We taste with our eyes first. That's part of the reason we spread the meal out, so it's not chaos for our senses. You really appreciate each dish for its merits. Think you can keep up with the Samuels family, Miss Sierra?"

"I'll certainly give it the old college try." That's what my grandpa always said. He says it more now that three of his grandchildren are in college.

"That's the spirit. Now, wouldn't you prefer to spend time with your roommate? Zoe can introduce you to some of the family. I need to preserve the secrecy of my recipes. Don't want you taking any of these across the border to your heathenish Canadian family." She wags the spoon at me, but sparkles in her eyes belie the harsh tone.

I think she's half kidding, which means she's also half serious. I'm not sure which part is serious, but I suspect I'm in her way more than anything, so I finish my pumpkin bread and toss the paper plate in the trash on my way out of her kitchen.

"Did Mother treat you right?" Zoe asks, sitting on the laps of two boys who I assume are her cousins, because she has a picture of her immediate family in the dorm, and she only has two sisters.

"She explained what to expect. And I was allowed to have an appetizer."

"Because you didn't eat breakfast when I told you to." Zoe

pokes me in my belly. "Sierra, this is Duke and Mattie."

"Matt," the boy on the right says.

"Mattie. They're my cousins and cousins to each other. I've been sitting on them since we were kids. It's a Thanksgiving tradition."

"Only if you pay our medical bills." Duke grins at me, though he winces when Zoe punches his arm too hard, like a sister punches a younger brother.

When they were kids, the boys were probably tiny, but now they dwarf Zoe. Duke looks like he plays basketball, and Mattie looks like he swims. They're both in college, too, but they go to state schools, while Zoe and I go to a private university. I appreciate the view, but I don't like how my brain slows down at the sight of them, although it seems to amuse Duke plenty.

I sit down across from them on an empty section of ottoman, weirded out by the fact there's someone behind me, but the woman adjusts so that all I feel is her warmth at my back.

"You like dogs?" Duke indicates the dog show with his chin.

I nod. "I like the working dogs best."

At least the dog show gives me something to look at, but once it's over, there's only the pre-game, and if there's anything more boring than sports, it's talking about sports without the game even on. Which means it's time for the usual merry-go-round of questions adults ask college students, plus those they ask international students. My interrogators seem endlessly fascinated, but after the forty-seventh interview, I'm about ready to break and tell them whatever they want to know if they just ask a new question.

What's your major?

Geoscience and environmental science.

Wow, that sounds involved. Is it difficult?

Sometimes.

Does it require a lot of math?

Sometimes. I like math.

You're going to put me out of a job.

What's your job?

Oil.

There are lots of oil people in the room, which is no surprise to me. I reassure them, disingenuously, that I'm not going for their jobs and that lots of environmental scientists also look into improving the viability and safety of extracting fossil fuels. That's not what I want to do, though. I'm more concerned about rising sea levels. But although I'm passionate about my subject, I've learned from years of extended family dinners that talking about the importance of climate science is a great way to drag down the mood of a room. No one wants doom and gloom before yams.

What year are you in?

I'm in my freshman year. I'm Zoe's roommate.

And where are you from?

Oakville, outside Toronto.

Oh, Canada!

Yes, that's how the song goes. (I don't actually say that.)

Do you have Thanksgiving there?

We have the first Thanksgiving, but it's not as big of a deal there, and it's at the beginning of October, when all of you are putting up your twelve-foot skeletons.

Do you speak French?

I speak tourist French. Do you speak Spanish?

Only through high school.

How does it feel to be in America?

Different.

Different how?

Lots of little ways. We've got a lot in common, but then sometimes you Americans do something that makes my brain short-circuit. Then I put gravy and curds on fries, so you think I'm the weird one.

Why don't you say 'eh?'

Why don't you say 'howdy?' (That one, I say out loud.)

That's for ranchers and cowboys. We say 'y'all' and 'bless your heart.' You know what that means, right?

(After checking that Mother and anyone else with gray in their hair isn't listening) Fuck you and the horse you rode in on?

That one gets me a laugh. After a while, with enough bad questions, you learn to entertain yourself.

Zoe gets some of the same questions about college, presumably from people she sees less often. She navigates these familial waters more easily than me. This isn't the only venue in which I envy her—not just for having family so close and so loving but for the comfort that familiarity grants her, while I'm swimming against their current like a different species altogether. At school, too, where she makes friends so fast that they're *all* good friends, practically family. The only reason why I'm here with her today is because I'm the one the university paired with her by lottery.

She weaves between cousins and aunts and uncles and adopted family and their guests as though they're all the same breed, of the same kind. She remembers her aunt's birthday, congratulates an older cousin's promotion, jumps for joy with an aunt before complimenting the engagement ring and assuring her future uncle that he's already part of the family, although she looks forward to inducting him more formally. Apparently, the two have been dating for a while and he's been to five family Thanksgivings.

Strangers are friends and friends are family, and she's one of the threads binding them, charming and bubbly and beautiful—the blueprint for the kind of person that I wish I were. Zoe climbs mountains; I'm happier in a warm bathrobe with a mug of hot chocolate.

Duke tries to converse with me, and I try to answer his questions like everyone else's, but he gets better answers from Zoe when she rescues me, her arm around my shoulders as she tells him all the things she's done during her freshman year. Duke keeps the warmth of his gaze on me, but it's Zoe's proximity that convinces the stiff creakiness of my joints to loosen.

However, seeing her in her native habitat strikes home that these people have such a deeper and richer context of knowledge of her than me. I know she's more of a night owl than me but that she also seems unaffected by early classes. I know she likes MoonPies and nachos with cheap queso. I know her bookshelf in our room boasts an eclectic collection that defies categorization, because she's aiming for a comparative lit minor to go with her communications major. I know she goes out every Saturday night to parties on or off campus, but Friday nights, we curl up on her bed and watch a movie the way other people in our dorm go to church on Sunday mornings.

We became fast friends and soaked each other in since freshmen orientation, but as well as I think I know her, she's still a mystery.

I hide my frustration and the anger that tries to mask it. Her smile more than brightens the room despite the drawn drapes, while I wear the ever-ubiquitous *I'm fine* smile that fools parents across international borders on video chat and strangers right in front of me alike.

But I don't think I fool her. I'm more transparent to Zoe than she is to me. Being around her family gives me no further clues, because the family itself seems false in its own way. Maybe that's just how people are, whether at a family feast or ten-year high school reunion. They can't resist a performance.

And throughout Zoe's tapestry of conversation, into which she ropes me, throughout the stumbling of some guests, throughout the shrieking play of the children, throughout the occasional charged discussion accelerated by wine, Mother hustles and bustles through the kitchen alone.

It doesn't seem fair and goes against every ounce of feminism that rings through me, but two things keep me from bringing it up. The first is that my outrage is two degrees removed. This is not my house, and now is neither the time nor the place for a debate—despite other people's mild lack of couth.

The second is that *no one* but Mother works, despite the fact that the room is at least half women. I doubt the family expects such unsung industriousness from women so much as Mother won't let anyone else help her in the kitchen or contribute significantly to a feast that she considers her sole province. That I can respect, even if I don't understand how the rest of the family can just stand back while Mother does everything.

I almost regret coming to the Thanksgiving feast—regret tinged with hunger as the pumpkin bread reaches the end of its efficacy—when pre-game shifts into game and the room goes not just quiet but silent as Father switches the volume back up on the television.

Everyone turns toward the television as a military man in dress blues sings "America the Beautiful." Then they put their hands on their hearts as Kelly Clarkson sings "The Star-Spangled Banner." Even Mother's clatter in the kitchen ceases. She stands amid chaos of her own making with her hand on her heart, eyes sparkling. She's not the only one who sheds a tear. Kelly Clarkson sounds wonderful, of course, but their reactions disturb me much the way the recital of prayers and the Pledge of Allegiance do—like children's choirs singing in minor key.

I don't appear to be the only one confused, which is a comfort in and of itself. Other guests look around with some bewilderment before they put their hands on their hearts and regard the television with less convicted reverence. I do the same. I'm glad no one expects me to sing.

At the conclusion of the anthem, the family cheers with the players and audience on the screen. Then Father switches the television off, which darkens the family room further. Protests from guests as well as family members are a more raucous chorus.

Father holds up his hands, one with the remote and the other empty, as though he's about to pray over a baptism. "We'll watch the game after the feast. It's time to turn off your phones. It's also a good time to make your bets, while you're disconnected. Don't make us collect phones, and don't be the one who gets caught watching the game during one of the courses. I'm looking at you, Phil. You don't want to be the reason we can't have nice things."

Father points at a man who looks much like him, which probably makes him a brother or cousin. Phil holds up his phone in response, making a show of turning it off and sticking it back in his pocket.

I don't make a habit of shutting off my phone, but it's just another Thursday at home. Mom won't be expecting a call from me until Saturday or Sunday, and who else am I going to call?

After pulling my phone out of my purse, I consider just turning it to silent but think, irrationally, of hospitals and airplanes, where you're told that phones interfere with sensitive equipment. Even if it's not true, you turn it off just in case. And what's more sensitive than family during a holiday?

I turn my phone off.

"All right." Father's pose changes from that of a priest to an air traffic controller. "Kids upstairs for the kids' table in the theater room. And everyone needs to wash their hands. Full bathroom with a double vanity is through the right door in the family room, for those who don't know. The powder room is in the front of the house, if you need to use the bathroom. We're certainly not going to tie you to the table for ten hours, but you don't want to miss more than you have to. For those of you who are new to our feasts, we implore you to *really* wash your hands. We don't want anyone ruining the experience of Marcie's food, even on a molecular level, right?"

"Is he serious?" I ask Zoe in her ear so her hair can hide my incredulity.

"Semi. I mean, were you planning to *not* wash your hands after going to the bathroom?" Zoe wrinkles her nose, but she's much less serious than her father. She's well-acquainted with how I always need to pee before starting anything and how fast I go through hand soap in our shared suite bathroom.

I pinch her side, then hand her my purse so I can join the short line in the foyer. The powder room is like the rest of the house, cozy-wrapped emerald green wallpaper decorated with a watercolor floral print that was big in the nineties and has come right back around to trendy. The hand soap smells like good vanilla. I make sure to wash for thirty seconds, in case the person on the other side is counting with me.

Back in the den, I ask Zoe, "Are we at the kids' table or the adults' table?"

"Dealer's choice," Father says. His cheeks burn so floridly that he's either had a beer or he's as sensitive to heat as his wife and daughter are to light. He hugs his daughter again, kissing her head through her hair. "You're in that awkward place, aren't you? Between who you were and who you're going to be."

I know what he means. I hear versions of it a lot, but I think it's an oversimplification. I am who I am. Just because I'm in a transitional state doesn't mean I'm not whole and complete as I am. A chrysalis is an encapsulated, contained object, even if what's on the inside is unimaginable goo.

"You can stay down here with the fuddy-duddies talking about their jobs, or you can go upstairs and watch movies with the kids. The food is mostly the same, although there's less wine," Father says. "It's up to you."

"Oh, come on, Sierra." Zoe tugs on my arm. "We didn't come here to sit at the kids' table."

Honestly, Thanksgiving dinner and Disney movies doesn't sound like such a bad holiday to me, but that's the safe and secure me, the one whose horizons I'm trying to stretch. I nod and let Zoe drag me to sit near the bay window with some of the other younger adults and older teens. No one much younger than me, by fashion, fit, and accessories. In the midst of swift growth and genetic difference, it's hard to tell exactly.

The only reason I care is that everyone has wine glasses, including me, and no one's fetching them away from us. I push mine away from my setting.

Zoe pushes them back. "Don't worry. When they pour wine, it's the proper amount. They don't fill it halfway, much less to the brim. We're more generous with everything else. They're not trying to get you drunk, and you could probably use something to relax you. I can feel your tension through your thigh."

With all the people trying to fit together, we're leg to leg, body heat bringing a flush to my cheeks and ears. Too hot. I think again of the kids' table, even though I'm not a kid and the kids' table to me means knees sticking up in awkward directions—even though I haven't grown much taller than my twelve-year-old self, and a short table might actually suit my legs better. But Zoe and I are around the same height, and a bird's got to fall out of the nest eventually.

Besides, I could bathe in cinnamon, nutmeg, clove, and allspice, and when I close my eyes, there's still heat and closeness, but no one's a stranger, everything smells wonderful and homey, and I guess I can stay a little while longer—or a long while longer, given Mother's timeline.

The table goes quiet again. I open my eyes to everyone closing theirs and bowing their heads. This, at least, I've done before—as far as neutral compliance goes, it's the easiest thing in the world to fake. As long as the prayer isn't call-and-response or collectively spoken, it should stay out of the amorphous realm of 'common things that creep Sierra out.'

"Heavenly Father."

The prayer warrior is Mother, which I don't expect, just like I don't expect her at the head of the table, given Father's commanding tone from before. However, she's the one who made the multi-course meal, so as far as I'm concerned, Mother can do whatever she damn well pleases from here on out.

Zoe's older sister Layla sits at the foot of the table, next to Matt. The whole time we've been at their house, Layla has never looked up, and if she's spoken to anyone, I wasn't there to see it. Even now, she stares intently at her empty place setting, nostrils flaring. She doesn't meet Mother's eyes or her sisters' or Father's, nor cousins' nor guests'. She holds the arms of her dining room chair as though she's bound to them with jute.

"We gather here today to give thanks for the blessings You have bestowed unto us. We are humble people, Lord. We do not deserve our daily bread. We do not deserve our meat. We do not deserve the joy of fruits, vegetables, roots of the earth. We do not deserve the decadence of sweetness. We do not deserve spirits derived from fermentation. Yet You, O Lord, have not only blessed us with plenty, but You encourage us to partake of these blessings with grateful heart and bottomless hunger. Our cornucopia overflows, and for that we give thanks and praise."

Already, the blessing has gone on longer than I'm used to. When I went to my childhood friends' homes for dinner, most families wouldn't say grace at all—just tuck in. Some, though, did a little rhyme or song, something easy to pass down to their children and their children's children. I would bow my head and listen to their nursery rhymes, and that was that. One of my friends' family was more devout; the father gave thanks for the blessings of food and asked for God to use it to nourish our bodies and take care of us through the week. It felt intensely Christian to this godless heathen of a godless family, but also strangely Pagan. I didn't understand it, but I didn't dislike it.

I hadn't expected a sermon for a blessing. My stomach rumbles in the silence between Mother's words. Zoe pokes me with her elbow, and Duke snickers. But when I open my eyes a crack, no one glares at me for something I can't control, so I close my eyes again. I'm tired from small talk anyway. The biggest risk, aside from my stomach growling, is that the warmth of closeness lulls me to sleep.

"May You bless those who receive these blessings and, however self-serving it may be, bless the hands that prepared it. May this time of fellowship foster new friendships and family and be in the spirit of Your own feasts—when a boy's lunch became sustenance for a crowd, when You instructed us to be the salt of the earth, when wine and unleavened bread became Your own blood and broken body.

"May our hands understand the gifts they hold. May our mouths and bellies understand the luxury that sustains us. May our guts grant our bodies nutrients. May our minds remember You in soft bread, savory thighs, in milk and wine, in chocolate melting on our tongue. May we take for granted not one bite given to us. In Your holy name we pray."

Everyone concludes with 'amen,' including me, which again feels more Pagan than Christian to me, so it spills more honestly from my mouth, despite my disquiet. I thought that because Zoe doesn't go to church and doesn't say more than a silent grace when she eats, her family didn't truck seriously with religion, but she's certainly not the only freshman to ditch the faith in college.

After Mother finished cooking, she changed into a nicer shirt. Long, loose, swinging sleeves make a priestess of her as she instructs some of the men of her family to light candles every half-foot down the table and completely close all the curtains.

Others go to the kitchen for the large crockpots, the contents of which they ladle into stacks upon stacks of ceramic bowls. With hands gloved against the heat, they bring the bowls two by two, serving Mother and Father first, then on down the table to the younger adults. The room is no longer silent, but it remains solemn, like whispered memories during a wake.

One of the servers sets soup bowls in front of me and Zoe. I lean forward to breathe the perfume of olive oil and vegetable stock. When I reach for the soup spoon, Zoe covers my hand and shakes her head.

Wait until everyone is served.

Mother spreads her arms and holds her hands palm up, like a benediction.

This is much more ceremony than I'm used to with food, and we haven't even started. My stomach growls again. This time, the snickering among the younger set is louder, but Mother just smiles. A hungry stomach responding to her food compliments her, at least as prologue.

"For our first course to whet the appetite, we have jalapeño soup. I apologize to those of you who are sensitive to spice. This Southwestern soup has a bit of a kick for the untrained tongue."

As soon as Mother sits in her throne at the end of the table, everyone picks up their soup spoons—almost synchronized, and my heart jolts against their rhythm, disorienting as vertigo. But they sink the spoons into soup at different times, clinking metal against ceramic. I lift my own soup spoon, with Zoe's encouraging prod. After blowing on the lightly steaming broth,

I let the soup pour in a smooth slide down my throat.

It's still a little too hot, and for a moment, I think that's what's wrong, that I've burned my tongue and don't feel it yet. But I wait for about thirty seconds, watching everyone else, before taking another bite.

I taste almost nothing.

There's texture of mild roux, of blitzed carrot and jalapeño and scallion, sliced mushroom floating in the autumnal soup like fallen leaves. But aside from mild sweetness from the carrot and a savory note from olive oil, the soup is tasteless.

Usually, people tell me that something's mild, then I'm hit over the head with the frying pan of a flavor—beer and wine, butter added to movie theater popcorn, the spiciness of a novelty hot sauce. I've never been told that something's too strong, only for a flavor to be so delicate as to be indetectable. Especially in a part of the country known for its peppers, I'm quietly floored not to be bitch-slapped by a jalapeño seed.

She must have deseeded all her peppers, to a speck, then roasted them too much—flavor heaven to flavor purgatory. I don't cook much more than melting cheese on bread, in its various iterations, but watching cooking shows is self-care, and my own family's mistakes have at least taught me a few things about what I'm *not* supposed to do.

Maybe it's supposed to be mild, like a palate cleanser. Maybe Mother just wanted to warn the most sensitive to guard their tastebuds. Maybe she's fielded complaints against the spice level before.

I don't say anything, because that would be rude, but I do look around again to gauge family's and friends' reactions to the soup. After the flood of scents from the kitchen, I'm disappointed that the first course doesn't meet the promise of its fragrant prelude.

Some guests blink and look around with me, but not all. Perhaps the advice to abstain from appetizers serves to keen the tastebuds, and soda and pumpkin bread killed mine.

The family, however, drinks down their soup as though they haven't swallowed in days, including Zoe. Like to like, light sensitivity to light sensitivity, those born in and married in appear to share similar tastes. They're halfway through their soups before I make a dent.

I search the table instead of the faces around it. Our place settings have three kinds of drink glasses—one for water, one for white wine, one for red—smaller ceramic bowls, bread plates, and every utensil known to man. Centerpieces of evergreen branches, pinecones, acorns, and fake leaves weave among the candlesticks. There are no hot pads or other protections for the dining table against heat, presumably because food will be served rather than set out to be passed around.

There's also none of the staples of a dinner table, whether everyday or for special occasions. No condiments like mustard, mayonnaise, ketchup, hot sauce, butter, or honey; no gravy, sauce, or hummus; no cooked bacon bits; no dinner rolls; and no seasoning, including pepper mill or salt shaker. Even fast-food restaurants usually have sugar and sugar substitute, sometimes pepper, red chili flakes, and Parmesan—but always salt.

I lean over and whisper behind Zoe's hair again, "Who do

I ask to pass the salt?"

The quiet table goes silent, and not in reverence.

The family turns toward me, necks creaking and eyes unblinking. Their reaction alarms the other guests as much as me. My face is all eyes. My stomach still clenches, threatening to growl, but it would be more embarrassing this time, so I stiffen and pray my body disappears while all attention focuses upon me with uncanny intensity, like a bad high school movie cliché.

Mother sets her soup spoon on her bread plate. Her welcoming, warm smile curves down like melted wax into a frown. Only the sparkle in her eyes—from flickering candlelight, from life—convinces me that she is still there behind the exaggerated, cartoonish disappointment.

She stands, bracing her hands on either side of her utensils as though to hold herself back from crawling onto the table like an angry lion. "Who said they want salt?"

As though she can't follow the direction of everyone's gaze. Shame tightens an internal iron maiden around my chest, although I don't even know what I did wrong. She takes her sweet time finding me, though, looking down the line of people on either side of the tables until she reaches the end. Her attention slaps me into embarrassed mortification.

In that moment, I can imagine no greater nightmare.

As her interrogative gaze alights upon me, her frown does not soften, but she straightens, less looming, and lifts her chin. Her voice is soft, with what I think is kindness. "I suppose you must be forgiven. You're not of the family. I should have made the expectations clearer during our discussion. Or Zoe should have told you everything required before bringing you to our table."

Mother levels her stunning maternal glare upon her daughter, who appears more inured to its effect but not entirely unaffected. Her thigh tightens against mine.

"What I serve is what you eat. I've worked hard over the last week preparing these meals exactly as I intend them to be eaten. I will not have anyone insult me by requesting anything other than what is provided, as though what blessings flow are inadequate."

Everyone's still staring at me. Even those behind me burn holes into the back of my head. Mother is a high judge and I am small, with an audience of thousands silently condemning me to the gallows. Just when I think it can't get any worse, my vision swims.

I refuse to cry in front of so many strangers; biology disregards my wishes.

"It's exceptionally rude to require your hosts to allow you to alter the meal that they give you with the generosity of their time and effort. This isn't a restaurant where you can demand your meal to your satisfaction. This isn't a tailor, to adjust everything to your fit. You accept what you're given with a grateful heart, and you don't complain, because you're young. You don't know what good food is. You don't have the palate, and you don't have the experience. If you find yourself in need of salt, young lady, might I suggest those crocodile tears?"

"She's just a teenager." One of the guests shrugged with his spoon, his grimace approximating a smile. "Give the girl a break. She didn't know the rules. There's no reason to yell at anyone asking for a salt shaker. Pepper and salt are staples on most tables so people can season to taste."

"I make these dishes according to *my* recipes!" Mother slams both her hands on the table to punctuate each emphasized word. "*My* recipes. My *mother's* recipes. *Her* mother's recipes. These recipes have been perfected over decades. Blood, sweat, and tears have been poured into them, sometimes quite literally. I have burn marks on my arms from the oven, slice scars on my fingers from knives. I have cooked for my family when there was no heat, and I have cooked for my family when there was no air conditioning. In case it wasn't perfectly clear before everyone walked in today: If your mother taught you well, you will eat what I provide, every last drop, every last smear, and you will say thank you when you're done. Every element of every dish is sown with my love to feed the hungry, so you will not question my love, you will not question my spice, and you will not question my salt. Do you understand me?"

One might assume that Mother's vitriol directed away from me would be a relief, but I just fight not to sob harder as hot tears stream down my face. Some might even fall into the soup. My throat holds a million little rocks inside, and my vision narrows with bubbled focus on the man shrinking like me under Mother's swelling anger. The person who presumably brought him to the feast looks away as though he doesn't know him, which is more than Zoe does for me.

The man who did speak up can't meet Mother's eyes, but he nods. I don't blame him. My guts are in turmoil. Some cultures take taste more personally, which I know but don't understand when tongues taste so differently; self-seasoning isn't commentary on the feeder but the fed. When I entered a Texas red-brick redolent with Southern hospitality, I didn't expect to find such offense here.

Mother takes her throne once more, then gestures for the first course to proceed, although she clatters her soup spoon with more force against the side of her bowl.

The man who spoke up raises his head and looks at me. The sight of a young woman crying contorts his face with a clenching of teeth and the urge to cry himself. But he swallows thickly, Adam's apple bobbing sharply above his collar, and he indicates that I should eat, too.

Almost everyone avoids looking at me—the shunning of the outcast—unwilling to be associated and punished by proximity after witnessing the castigation of the last person who tried to help. I associate such behavior with high school, but maybe adults never really grow out of it.

The soup no longer steams. It's the perfect temperature, and my tears have seasoned it to my taste. I get the jalapeño now.

I consider taking my phone from my purse and contacting a rideshare to get out of here. On the way home, I'd pick up fried chicken with all the spice I could ask for. But I'm hungry, and I don't want to upset Zoe. I wish she were more forthcoming about what the feast would entail, though, before convincing me to come. Who wants a Thanksgiving with this many rules?

As soon as the last person sets down their spoon, Mother gestures for her servers to take the bowls away—her frown turned upside-down as though it were never there—then for them to bring covered bread baskets. The five family members go person by person, offering them a selection of croissants, Hawaiian rolls, and yeasted dinner rolls. None of the family takes more than one; two of the guests take two, and one of them takes one of each. The family server glares at them. Mother goes still, her bright, pale eyes unblinking, but she says nothing.

I select a croissant. I note no additional butter offered, nor jam, jelly, or marmalade. I put my croissant on the bread dish like Zoe and Duke next to me and wait for everyone to be served.

When Mother receives her bread and sits, the family begins to eat, and so do I.

The croissant is good. It needs nothing more.

"Pasquale, the wine, please." Mother points to the huddle of bottles on her hutch.

Pasquale, the youngest server but still at least thirty years old, gives Mother a bow like a sommelier. He disregards the wine brought by guests and instead opens the cabinet to pull out a white wine. He starts at the head of the table with Mother.

Zoe's right. He only serves a little, rather than filling up the smaller wine glass. The tang complements the bread, and the butter in the croissant counteracts the dryness of the wine. It's not bad, although I'd prefer ginger ale, and I'm still not fond of the alcohol burn at the back of my throat, nor how hunger through thin soup and a single small croissant makes that burn sink down my esophagus only to rise, as heat does, to my head.

I have no tolerance. If Mother is sensitive, this concerns me. I feel like I'll never talk again, but I still fear my own tongue.

"It's so quiet." But Mother doesn't chide. She speaks as though she's having a normal conversation. "Why don't we honor this special day by going around the room and saying what we're thankful for? I'll start, then George, then so on. I'm thankful for… I'm thankful that, despite bad weather and bad circumstances, the whole family could be here for Thanksgiving dinner. I'm thankful for the chance to feel full at the end of the day. I'm thankful for familiar and unfamiliar faces, for people who have been adopted into the family and people who have yet to be given that honor. I hope you know I would accept all of you here as honorary family, and you always have a roof over your head and a warm meal if you need it. George?"

Father coughs, stands, holds up his glass, which only has enough for a swallow. "I'm thankful for good food, good mood, and good friends. I'm thankful our house has been blessed another year and that we have the opportunity to share so many of those blessings with others." He swallows the last of the wine with a hum of appreciation, then takes his seat.

The man next to him—out of place in a clashingly formal suit and tie, more business finance than holiday—doesn't stand but holds his wine glass up. He stammers for a moment, on the spot unexpectedly, but he finds his footing with: "I'm thankful for generous hosts and for my health, even when other things are falling down around me."

Other people, family and guests, stand or raise a glass or both in their gratitude, the wine warming feelings. All thank the hosts. The tension from my faux pas melts away, but not the undercurrent of requirement.

From the bench, another man in a suit raises his glass. "I'm thankful that, despite a bad year, Ollie here helped me find another job, which gives me the health benefits I need."

"I'm thankful my small business continues to thrive, for the family's sake," one of Zoe's uncles says. "I was able to take on young Matt over there as an apprentice and hire two new employees."

"I'm thankful for the opportunity of this fine feast, for me and for my daughter upstairs. She's had it so difficult this last year." The young woman brushes away better tears than mine. "You don't know what this means to us."

"Before I met Alex, I thought no one could see me, much less come up and talk to me." Another young woman in a playful semi-formal gown stares down with adoration upon her husband. "He brought me out of my shell, and if you don't mind me mixing my metaphors, he watered this wallflower in front of everyone until I bloomed so brightly that they envied him when they ought to envy me. I'd be nowhere without Alexander Samuels."

"I'm thankful that my wife over here, Connie—the best daughter of a universally wonderful family—is blessing me with a daughter who I hope will be at least half as good as her. We've had many blessings this year, my new family. My heart is full." The man covers his heart and smiles as his wife kisses his flushed cheek.

I notice a pattern in everyone's thanks. The members of the family, born or added, are grateful for good fortune; the guests are grateful for the family's fortune shared. The sinking sensation in my abdomen differs from guilt, but it mimics the same visceral vertigo.

I can't say when this whole experience went off the rails, whether it's even off the rails, or if I just don't understand Americans—or even just this family. Was it when I came in? When Mother took me aside and dismissed my host gift? When everyone was told to wash their hands?

Was it when Mother and Father became Mother and Father to me as well? Was it Zoe's snickerdoodles—the family recipe, with sea salt sprinkled on top? Or was it when I first met Zoe and she told me she was glad that, of all the people she could have been paired with, she got the Canadian, because she was looking forward to making me say I'm sorry?

In the dark room lit by lights above the table, a few in the kitchen for servers to see by, and candlelight, the rest of the drape-blocked world falls away. I can't hear the kids upstairs, not their movie nor their laughter. I can't hear cars on the road, nor the groan of tree branches or rustle of fallen leaves in the frigid wind. There is only this room, this table, and a long ellipse of people giving rote thanks and kissing the ring.

I touch the cold screen of my dormant phone, but the speeches swing to the younger side of the tables.

"Layla?" Mother waves encouragement from the other end. "It's your turn, sweetheart. What are you thankful for?"

Layla looks up. She's eaten her soup and her bread and drunk her wine, but she doesn't raise a glass nor does she stand from her throne, still invisibly bound in place. "I'm thankful for atypical antipsychotics."

Duke and Matt snort. Matt still has wine in his mouth, and it comes out his nose, spraying his empty plate. He quickly dabs it away. Zoe bites her lip and pushes her mouth into a frown very much like Mother's, except I think it's to keep from grinning, while Mother's lips melt her smile away.

"What about you, Zoe?" Mother asks.

Zoe stands and raises her glass, which, like Father's, only has a swallow left. "I'm thankful to have a good friend in my new roommate, Sierra. Getting assigned at random could have been a nightmare. Instead, I got someone smart, sweet, and so generous in her own way. I'm really glad she can be here today."

I want to hate her for bringing me here and making me a part of this ritual. I want to hate her for not telling me what's going on. I want to hate her for saying that a person shouldn't be alone over the holidays while the campus is so empty. I want to hate her for the confusion in my stomach and my throat, the dryness on my tongue, the tears that left trails on my cheeks and still sting my eyes. I want to hate her for all the eyes on me.

But when she throws back her head and swallows and looks down at me with that smile lighting up her whole face, bright as her unnerving pale eyes, I can't hate her, and I think all this might be strange, but that doesn't mean it's bad. It's Thanksgiving. Everyone's saying what they're thankful for. Isn't that what Americans do? And if Mother is a little rigid, we all have our quirks. It's my job as a guest to respect the hosts' wishes, as long as they're reasonable. Providing seasoning and condiments is reasonable and normal, but another reasonable normal is not insulting the host's food.

Zoe sits back down. My turn.

I try to stand, but it's difficult to get out from an unmoving bench, especially with my short legs. I catch my calf on the front of the bench, teeter back, then out of control. The bench relinquishes my leg too late. I crash against the wall, then struggle to regain my balance.

"My roommate, everyone," Zoe jokes, but she grabs my arm to help me right myself. Duke reaches out, too, but Zoe helps me before he can. "Easy on the wine."

"I just lost my balance." It's silly that I feel the need to explain my clumsiness, but I can't even look down the table toward Mother's piercing eyes, for fear they'll bear the same judgment. "I shouldn't have stood, but now I'm up, so I guess I'll…" I force myself to stop babbling, swallow my own gathered saliva, and try to salvage the situation, if not my dignity. "I'm thankful for… I'm thankful for…"

I had the whole other half of the table to think of what to say. I *had* something to say, but the fall jostled it right out. My brain is a blank whiteboard, with nothing but the unreadable smears of old thoughts. It doesn't help that I'm afraid of what might happen if I don't say anything I'm thankful for. I *have* plenty to be thankful for. I don't know why it's so hard to find even one with everyone's attention back on me. My lip threatens to tremble.

Then I remember the pattern. I don't have to overthink this. I don't have to come up with something unique or thrilling. They already got their pound of flesh—or pinch of salt—from me. Boring is best anyway.

"I'm thankful for my roommate, too. When I chose our

university, I wanted to get as far away from home as humanly possible, but I didn't realize how much I'd miss them. I was honored when she invited me to her family's Thanksgiving experience. So I'm grateful to our hosts, and I'm thankful for Zoe, for convincing me to take risks but also giving me so much comfort when my family feels so far away, while hers is so close."

"Awww. How sweet." Zoe rubs my arm as I work my way back onto the bench. Getting in is easier than getting out, which feels like a metaphor. I'm acutely more aware of Zoe's leg against mine on one side and Duke's on the other, and my face heats again.

Safely ensconced on the bench, I drink the rest of my wine, which seems to be the trend, if not a constant.

Duke raises his glass without standing. "I'm thankful that our basketball team went all the way to the championship last year. We didn't win, but we made a mark, and I think this coming season will finally be our year. I'm also thankful that this wonderful Thanksgiving feast has given us the opportunity to meet new people and make new friends." He does a one-sided cheer with an invisible glass over my plate setting, then finishes his wine.

My cheeks and ears threaten to catch the drapes on fire. So much about this day is unprecedented. I don't know how normal it is for everyone else in the room, but it's disorienting as culture shock for me, similar to what I experienced coming all the way down here. Not so much the Canadian/American culture shock. I've been to America before; we're not *that* different. It was my independence, the change in my routine, in environment and community. And here in this room, I have an equally disorienting awareness that there are whole small worlds outside of the university, too, all as reelingly different as the one I arrived in four months ago.

The thanksgiving continues down the tables until they reach Mother again.

She raises her glass. Father raises his glass. Both of their glasses are empty. Everyone's glass is empty, family and guests. The family raises their empty glasses, and so do the guests by their cue. For some of us, it takes a few beats longer, but Mother is patient, staring into the distance like a propaganda poster until every empty glass gleams under the dining room lights.

"We give thanks!" Mother declares.

Then she brings her glass to her mouth and spits a thick wad of saliva into the dregs.

The family follows suit, an echoing surround-sound of expectoration like a cavalcade of camels in a baseball dugout. Some are more substantial than others. I don't think anyone hocks a loogie or anything, but if the bench weren't sturdy, catching behind the knees, I might have jerked back all the way off my seat.

This is what separates the family from the guests like nothing else has, because horror rises in the eyes of the lost, the kind of horror reserved for people who pick their nose in public. Not even Mother's humiliation of me was enough to put them off the current of the feast. I'm adjacent enough to a snot-nosed kid that maybe they convinced themselves that Mother's annoyance was justified. Collective spitting throws them all off their best behavior. I'm not the only one who recoils, but a few guests are more successful than me, falling off the bench onto the rug or the tile. Harder to excuse strangeness when it directly affects you.

Not impossible, just harder.

The room erupts into low murmurs and harsh whispers as the family draws their guests back into place to persuade them to spit in the cup like the rest of them. We don't even get ancestry information as a reward.

Zoe hands me my glass. "It's okay."

"Zoe…"

"It's okay." She shows me how she's spit in her own glass.

It's the weirdest peer-pressure ritual I've ever been part of, but I tell myself that far classier people than me spit during wine tastings. I tell myself it's not hurting anything. I try to telepathically tell the other guests who look to me with the same wild-eyed confusion that it isn't weird *enough* to protest, that they were fine with a grown woman yelling at a teenager about salt, so saliva probably shouldn't be their line in the sand.

I gather what I can from a dry mouth and spit into the glass. It slides slimily down the side to mingle with what's left of the wine in a way that makes me uncomfortable.

"They're not going to make us drink fruit punch at the end, are they?" I ask Zoe.

Zoe laughs. "God, Sierra, no. You're so silly."

I'm the silly one here? But I set down my glass.

One by one, the guests do the same. It's not like they don't leave backwash every time they drink.

Mother raises her spit-bottomed glass once more. "One of the most wonderful things about getting together during the holidays is how much closer we become with each feast. In a world that does everything it can to separate us—by religion, work, class, caste, color—may we intentionally bring ourselves closer to friends, to family, to strangers, until we realize we are one."

She passes the glass to Father, and Father passes his glass to the person next to him.

"Now, wait just a minute…" Someone else stands, an older man in a fall-themed sweater over a collared shirt. "You want us to drink from someone else's glass? That has their spit in it?"

"We pour another glass of wine," Mother says, as though that's an answer.

"No. This is unacceptable. I don't know who's incubating a cold—or a cold sore. I'm not sharing wine glasses with anyone. No. This isn't okay."

"Leslie, think of how many people you've kissed. Parents and siblings when you were younger, certainly lovers as you grew up." Mother follows the progress of two servers— strapping cousins—as they round the table to stand behind the protesting man where he can't see, too shocked by Mother's demands to realize he's been flanked. My stomach growls again, but not in hunger. The sensation is too cold for that. "Consider carefully how much spit you've swapped over the years. There's plenty of evidence to show that kissing blends biomes and strengthens the immune system. This is no different, and with the addition of wine, I promise it will taste sweeter."

"No. I'm not okay with this. I'm sorry, Phillipa, but I need to leave. I can't stay for the rest of this." Leslie backs away from the table, but the young men behind him grab his arms just below his shoulders.

"Our ways may seem strange to you, but I promise there's method to our madness. And it's rude to leave the table of a host so early. I'm almost inclined to take offense." Mother gestures the other servers toward the hutch for another bottle of wine—white again.

"Zoe…" I murmur again, an otherwise wordless plea that this all make some kind of sense, that everything's going to be okay, because the cold dread spirals lower and lower, cold also in my hands and feet, even while my cheeks and ears flush red for reasons other than attraction or fluster.

She weaves her arm in mine as she passes her glass to me, then takes my glass and passes it down to Duke, who passes his to the uncle next to him. "It's okay. It's nothing. It's okay."

The servers pour the next wine. Its scent stings my nose. I watch it mingle with Zoe's spit with the same strange discomfort and ever-drying mouth. I lick my lips. I don't know what to say. Even with my limited frame of reference of what's socially acceptable, what's *polite*, I'm at a loss, with no context—modern or historical—for what's happening.

"You want to talk rude?" Leslie wrenches from the servers' hold. They let go but still block him so that he can't back away, and they poise their hands to grab him again if he tries. "Forcing everyone to follow your little traditions that make no sense, holding people hostage to your feelings, making them fawn over you in the name of decorum. But there's no world in which spitting and compelling someone else to drink it is normal. It's not even cute. I'd say I'm sure you're all very nice people, but now I'm not so sure. All I know is that I don't want to stay here anymore. I'm going home, getting Chinese takeout, and watching the fucking game."

He backs into the servers, then throws an elbow when he hits well-muscled walls—not quite bouncer or wrestler, but their fitted shirts delineate defined arms and chests. Leslie is no slouch himself, but he's no match for Mother's boys. When he thrashes against their hold, they dig dented shadows into his sweater and force him up and back onto the bench.

"No one leaves once the feast begins," Mother says, unfazed. "No exceptions. That's just common courtesy."

"Fuck, lady, you're crazy."

"That's no way to speak to Mother," says Phillipa, the woman who must have invited Leslie to the feast. She leans away from him in disgust and secondhand humiliation. "Not only is it unkind to throw accusations like that out there, insulting people with real problems, but she's been nothing but welcoming to you. Do you talk to *your* mother like that? You disappoint me."

"You're crazy, too. You're all crazy." Leslie's knee slams against the table, jostling the place settings, glasses, and candles. The family all jumps to ensure none of the candles or glasses tip over and readjust the garlands to their original position as the servers curl their arms around Leslie's neck and arms, effectively strait-jacketing him.

Mother sets down her glass as the servers reach her and

pour the new wine. "I know holidays can be stressful, but there's no need to resort to abuse. You're ruining the experience for all the other guests of my home. They came here for a nice meal, something they might not get at home, a different kind of experience, and you're interrupting that. You're also throwing us off schedule. The longer we spend arguing over the courses, the later we end up having to watch the game, even if we fast-forward through all the commercials. I'm sorry, but I can't let this assault on my hospitality go unanswered."

After the servers finish with the wine—including the glass in front of Leslie, knocked off its place from his struggles—the servers bring trays of charcuterie, raw veggies, and air-fried buffalo wings. They serve the same portions of everything to everyone, without asking if some people don't like salty meat or if they want a wing or a drumstick or if they don't like the texture of celery.

They skip over Leslie.

Mother leaves the table for the kitchen. She wheels one of the heavy butcher block islands behind Leslie.

Zoe… I'm not certain if I say it out loud, if it gets stuck in my throat like a toad, or whether it's just so loud in my head that I think I hear it. Nothing but her name in my mind and my mouth, because there's not enough room for anything else, certainly not words, given the elephant in the ivory cave—little more than simple, bloated disbelief, even in the face of what I see and know.

I tighten my arm around Zoe's to draw myself closer to her, away from Leslie and from Mother. Or maybe she tightens hers to keep me on the bench like the boys pinion Leslie.

Phillipa and the man on Leslie's other side climb out from the bench to give the two servers and Mother room. White encircles Leslie's irises, accentuated by bulging within sockets darkened not by genetics but stark, bloodless shock in his cheeks. The harder he struggles, the harder the servers hold, and they have the better position and greater strength.

The server holding Leslie's arms shifts his grip to grab Leslie's right wrist. Then the server slams the man's forearm onto the butcher block on his left. It's an awkward angle for Leslie, across his body. He groans, leans into the demand to ease the protest ache, but that puts him in a worse position to muster what strength he has. When Mother fortifies the server's hold with her own, pinning his hand to the block, he has no leverage to pull away.

"What— What are you doing? What do you think you're— No, no, please. Please, don't. I don't understand. Please, stop, don't, don't—"

He can't form coherent thoughts but makes his wishes known well enough in the blather. The whites of his eyes turn red, his voice quavering with the plea of a seven-year-old under threat of a spanking—a humiliating regression, but I don't think anyone judges him for it, especially when Mother retrieves the cleaver from her collection of knives off the butcher block.

He's not the only one asking broken questions. Other guests stand, try to run, yell, scream.

"What are you doing?"

"Stop! Stop, don't..."

"Please…"

That might be me, too, a spill of reasonable protests like piss down the leg of the fearful. But I don't think any of us, including Leslie, really think it's going to happen, even as the family stops us from running, holds us down, tells us to calm ourselves, that everything's okay, that we need to *stay* until the feast is complete.

The grandfather clock in the family room ticks its ponderous pendulum, but it only reads a little past two-thirty. Just thirty minutes at the table, to end at midnight.

There's never been a time when I wasn't in this darkened den, with interrogation lights above me and fire hazards lining the tables. Skin stretches over my skull, as though my scalp threatens to split and slough right off.

I can't believe what is happening, what I see, which is why I do nothing to stop it as Mother swings the cleaver down to thud on the butcher block.

Blood spurts in an arc from the arm. It misses Mother and the table, splattering instead against the partition between the kitchen and the family room. Leslie screams, high-pitched, without dignity. Mother only made it through half the wrist bones. The butcher block embraces the cleaver at an angle. She grunts as she rocks the blade back and forth. Leslie screams to the same rhythm, then once more as she jerks the cleaver free. Blood drips from the blade and spills rather than spurts onto the butcher block. Even though I can't blink, I still try to convince myself that it's red wine, because that makes more sense than what happened.

Another swing, with the deadly accuracy of someone who

has cut the head off a thousand chickens. The hand flops away from the wrist, limp in a soup of blood. Mother's long bell sleeves are stained wet and dark at their ends, but the color goes with the autumnal design.

She sets the cleaver to the side, then goes to the hooded stove. She takes one of the cast-iron frying pans from its place and rests it on an empty burner, which she switches up to high.

"Oh, God! Oh, God! Oh, God!" If it weren't for the screeching note of terror, it could have been a porn vid. Such supplication, even if he doesn't invoke the right gender.

Mother puts a silicone handle on the frying pan to take it off the heat, then brings it with conviction to the block, where the server forces Leslie's arm up. Mother stops the blood with a slam and fajita sizzle. It smells like grilled steak, hair burning in a curler, curdling myoglobin, tarnished pennies.

Leslie loses his words and screams even higher than before. I worry his eyes will pop out. His uvula jerks behind a wriggling tongue. No one tries to stop Mother now. What's done is done, and we're all caged by the family as well as by our own shock and self-preservation.

Mother doesn't stop with cutting off Leslie's hand. She takes another knife, much smaller, and cuts a line up the palm, slicing through life and love, to the third finger. Then, without the slightest squeamishness, she degloves the disembodied hand, not in one smooth motion but several, like undoing sheets from the bed and cases from the pillows. What's left is bone, muscle, tendon, ligament, fat, gristle, and dribbling vessel.

She superficially wipes it off with a tea towel, staining the cloth like a Halloween prop, then beckons for Leslie's empty dinner plate. One of the family within reach presents it to her with the flourish of a grand favor.

Mother throws the hand onto the plate in place of the casual hors d'oeuvres on everyone else's. With a pointed look at me, she grabs her flaky salt pot and sprinkles a generous amount all over what would have been the back of his hand, knuckles white gravestones between now twitching muscles, which she sets, smiling, in front of Leslie. Then she takes a spare hair band from her pocket, matching the one holding her hair back, and doubles it over Leslie's wrist, although he no longer bleeds much where the pan cooked him.

Although he's still screaming, the frequency has lowered to a different kind of agony—bone-deep and bereft with something taken that cannot be taken back. Amid pain are veins of horror, the steaming stump in plain view and impossible to deny, although the brain does what it can and pretends for odd seconds that the absence is a blind spot.

Mother meticulously washes her hands but doesn't remove her shirt, so the sleeves continue to smear her skin.

His hand still twitches with salt as though trying to escape.

She returns to her place at the head of the table. "Finger food, everyone. And remember, I expect you to clean your plate. That's the only way to conclude this course and move on to the next. Leslie here has an opportunity for the rarest of meat. You'll find it a bit tough, but I advise you to swallow what you cannot chew. There is, as always, water and wine. The good thing about finger food is that it's okay to get a little messy. Dig in."

The family members who don't have guests to hold start immediately, humming from the deliciousness of the first substantial food of the feast so far.

"You can't— This is ridiculous." I try to protest more vociferously, but I'm not strong enough to be heard past Duke and Zoe.

"It's all right, Sierra. Look, the only thing you have to do is follow the rules." Zoe thinks she's being reassuring. She's using her reassuring voice. And under other circumstances, it would, indeed, reassure. But a man's severed, skinned hand is dancing on his plate from the salt causing contractions to make it seem as alive as a migrating red crab. "She could have given him his hand with no seasoning at all."

"Seriously? Seriously?" Dogs hear me. I'm not sure Zoe does, but she can always read my lips.

"Eat, drink, be merry, and don't try to run. Those are the only rules. All you have to do is not break them."

"How am I supposed to eat, drink, and be merry when there's no escape?"

"If you eat, drink, and be merry, why would you want to escape? Look, the feast can get a bit…weird, but it doesn't have to be dangerous."

"Your mother chopped off a man's hand and is feeding it to him, uncooked." As though the fact it's raw is the real crime. "I want to escape."

"Well, you can't, so you might as well be merry." Zoe strokes my hair, trying to get me to calm down the way she did when I thought I was going to bomb my history midterm, because I love numbers but dates give me trouble, context has an endless number of variables, and I simply cannot be trusted to give a concise or coherent perspective. She brought me hot coffee from the student center and soothed me through my anxiety. And she thinks that's going to calm me down now while one of the servers holds the skinning knife to Leslie's neck as a sharp, looming threat to do as he's told.

"Why'd you bring me here, Zoe? I thought I was going to have a normal American Thanksgiving dinner. I didn't know it would be dinner with the Hewitts."

"Well, sweetie, this *is* Texas." Zoe seems more amused than insulted by the comparison, maybe because she's the one who introduced me to the original and the remake. "No, Mother just has her way of doing things. Otherwise, it's the same as anyone's Thanksgiving."

"I'm pretty sure they don't play gangland Truth or Consequences during their dinner."

"There are always consequences to everything," she says. "Some worse than others. You know that. If you fail a class, you'll probably be fine, but if you fail five, you need to leave school. If you take one road instead of another, you might get hit by a car or pick up a hitchhiker. I wanted you to come to our Thanksgiving so you wouldn't be lonely and so you could have some good comfort food."

"I can get good comfort food at Cracker Barrel, Zoe!"

"No. Real comfort food is home cooked. Restaurants try to mimic that, but it's all plastic and too much sugar and salt for soul. Maybe I should have explained how different this was going to be, but…I guess, for me, it's not different, you know?" She rests her head on my shoulder, still stroking my hair, and I can't help it. I'm calming down, at the mercy of memory and biofeedback despite the whimpering of the rolling-eyed man or the shock of the other guests that tells me I'm right to be shocked as well.

Just follow the rules. "What if I don't know what the rules are?"

"Mother knows you don't know the details, but you know the basics, so now you know better enough. As long as you do as I do or as Duke does, you'll get a good meal out of the night. You'll be one of us, part of our family, and all that entails. You'll always have a port in the storm, and your enemies will never prosper. That's what we offer, whether you're married in, born, or adopted. That's why I brought you here. Because I like you."

I close my eyes. I don't understand her. I don't want to understand her. She's not an idol fallen; if anything, her pedestal has risen higher, beyond perception. I don't understand how she could bring me into this, put me at this risk of humiliation and dismemberment because she *likes* me, because she thinks of her quiet, shy, horror-loving, mathy roommate as family. What kind of family does this to anyone? What kind of family thinks other people want to be part of a family like that?

Yet, adopted, married, and born, they fill two long dining room tables, and people keep marrying in without significant enough hesitation to keep them from the feast. A man's hand is a reasonable price for Mother's food, which they dig in to with gusto. And now, some guests creep back to their seat and pick at their plate, from similar urgings to what Zoe gives me.

Because they don't want their hands severed, either. They look away from the man who regards his twitching hand with nightmarish disbelief. They don't see him, like they don't see a misbehaving toddler in a grocery store or a homeless woman on the curb.

It's easier to eat when you don't see.

I feel for the edge of my plate and take a roll of what looks like prosciutto. After the blandness of the soup, the salt in the meat hits the snail of my tongue, yet it's the strongest taste I've had all night, and I keep my eyes closed to savor.

"Good girl," Zoe whispers. "Everything's going to be okay. If you're not sure, ask me or Duke. I won't steer you wrong. I never have before."

She's not perfect, but the salt awakens hunger, soothes the nausea. When I'm sure I can keep that roll of cured meat down, I choose salami next. Then the bursts of salty brine in the olives. Then the savory heat of home-fried wings. And to freshen my palate, I drink wine laced with Zoe's saliva, swallowing thickly. It all goes down better than I think it will, even as I steal glances at the condemned man forced to regard the reality of biting his knuckles.

A bead of blood gathers at the tip of the peeling knife at his neck, and the man fumbles at the plate, grabbing his hand and bringing it to his mouth with a gag and a sob.

"At our table," Mother says, halfway through her wings, in answer to the unspoken question from those of us who don't know better, "it's acceptable to spit out pits and bones. Traditional etiquette is that, if you need to remove food from your mouth, you use the same means used to put the food in.

A fork, a spoon, fingers, but as long as we're spitting fluid, feel free to spit phalanges. Finger food is much more casual. Of course, most of the bones in a finger are small enough to swallow, so if you don't want yourself to go to waste, I won't stop you from taking your calcium."

The man tears the meat from his twitching fingers, although his face is sloppier than mine with mucus and tears, because the knife at his throat tells him not to pause to use his napkin. With each bite, he swallows resignation that there is no reality, no road, in which he will ever get his hand back— not masticated to then dissolve, not with fragmented fingernails chewed off and picked from his teeth to set on the edge of the plate. Not when he slowly reduces the meat down to skeleton hand.

When there's too much meat still left beyond the reach of teeth alone, he looks to Mother, who stares like a marble statue with glass eyes until he breaks the hand apart to chew closer to the bone.

The server removes the knife from his neck when his plate is a mound of bones, nails, and gristle and his mouth is a stain of blood, tears, and snot. At Mother's direction, Phillipa, with some reluctance, wipes his face with his napkin so that he has some semblance of composure. Semblance alone—the man sees God and ghosts in his thousand-yard stare as he holds his arm against his bloodstained shirt.

"George, would you be so kind as to fetch an oxycodone pill from our medicine cabinet? I think there's still some left from your ACL surgery." Mother pats Father's shoulder as he stands.

The unspoken love between them requires no kiss to her head, no smile, no words. They've been matriarch and patriarch of this family—Mother and Father to all—for long enough to earn the respect of younger and elder alike. Their parents are next to them, salt-and-pepper hair and silver garland, proud of their family's strength.

How does this happen? How do two families like this find each other? How do they grow? Are they legacies in the area? Are their traditions like bloodline feuds, passed down generation to generation, inbred and bred out? Did his family know her family? Did they adopt each other like they adopt outsiders? I'm not an anthropologist, sociologist, or psychologist. I don't know how subcultures like this hatch from the frontal lobe of human beings, not just once but twice, four times, eight, with every split and entwinement of branches.

Father returns with a pill. The server pours fresh water into Leslie's water glass. Father hands the pill to Leslie, who snatches it greedily and swallows it like he swallowed some of his bones. He's not in as much pain as I think he should be. I suspect shock—both biological and psychological—has some effect, but the cook's cauterization might play a part, too. With a bad enough burn, the kind that destroys nerves, I think you stop being able to feel pain. I wonder, though, if he still feels his fingers, and if they itch.

"You'll feel better in no time. I can't speak to appetite, but the hand is about as meaty as a wing. It shouldn't have spoiled your dinner." Mother spits in her empty glass, and now the rest of us know what to do. Including Leslie.

We finish our wine and spit, then pass it to the next person, leaving the life map of two people in the glasses this time. Already, it doesn't seem so strange, and I recognize the desperate need of my scrabbling brain to make this normal, to make it nothing. I can hardly believe it, but that's the crux of the problem. It's so unbelievable that, like a dream, my mind struggles to thread a line of sense.

I shouldn't be able to justify this, yet all I can think is: *Just don't break the rules, and you'll be fine.*

You can get used to a hurricane if you never hit the eye. Just when you think your brain is going to break, it insists on resilience; I feel disorientingly sane. People like to pretend crazy does the most damage, but in the end, crazy has only a small reach. The worst things in the world are accomplished by the sane who people try to pawn off as monsters.

I clean my plate, too, but for the bones.

The servers go by each plate and take away the leavings with latex gloves into plastic bags that they store in a container in the kitchen that doesn't necessarily look like a trash can to me. Perhaps, as with every feast for such a large number, they expect an unwieldy amount of waste. Their choice of how and where to throw away their leftover bones is the least of my concerns. I have enough to deal with at the table.

When they're finished emptying the plates, they pour red wine into the clean larger wine glasses. I don't anticipate that they'll stay sanitary for long. I like the smell of the red wine better, and it's wetter on my tongue, more robust but with a less prominent alcoholic burn. I'm more concerned than ever about my lack of tolerance.

I wonder if our hosts silently design our rebellion.

Mother stands, swirling her wine glass then taking a deep whiff of the bouquet. I don't, and neither does Zoe; it's not part of the ritual to appreciate the wine right, as long as we appreciate it at all.

"This is, by far, the most beloved course among family and friends alike. You'll never see this in foodie culture, but we all know that this is what the people really want."

Those familiar with Mother's Thanksgiving feasts are already smiling, their teeth blinding under the bright table lights, their tongues thick and glistening in flickering candlelight. The servers approach with large casserole dishes, protected against the heat with cozies in old-fashioned patterns. It's unbearably domestic, unmistakably home cooked, like something for the grief-stricken or bedridden or for a potluck.

Even though my mom doesn't have a casserole dish to call her own, it causes an unexpected pang of nostalgia—not for a memory but for a wish, a wish I thought would be fulfilled tonight and instead has twisted from wholesome to inhumane. Yet the pang remains.

At each setting, the servers spoon a teacup serving of three different potato dishes: potatoes au gratin, roasted yams with marshmallows, and truffle mashed potatoes, with the last server following behind to dip a craterful of giblet gravy into the center. They go through one and a half dishes of each.

"I know it's tempting to have more," Zoe whispers, cool through the curtain of my hair, "but remember that you eat *only* what's served to you. There are no seconds. We're just four courses in and you need room for all the rest. But it's easily the best one. Savory, cheesy, and sweet, all on one plate. She does collect garage-sale Tupperware containers all year so that she can give away leftovers at the end of the day, though."

If I make it that far.

The potatoes smell really good, though, significant contributors to the rich, multilayered fragrance that fills the house and hits my nose-blind sense with fresh whiffs.

Mother adjusts her napkin, then groans with satisfaction from her first bite of mashed potatoes and gravy.

She's not the only one. Exclamations supporting her first impression rise all around the table like steam vents. After I spoon up some of the mashed potatoes, I join them in expressing how delicious it is.

Just the right amount of truffle oil that it doesn't taste like mothballs in an antique chest. Just the right amount of gravy that there's enough for every bite and not much left to gather afterward. There's at least three different kinds of cheeses in the potatoes au gratin, possibly five, from melty to earthy, and the marshmallows on top of and mixed in with the yams are perfectly caramelized with brown sugar. It was practically a dessert that would be too sweet if they gave us any more, but that's exactly what I want—more. I want a whole other plate, possibly two or three. We don't even have to continue with the other courses. The potatoes will do just fine all the way through to midnight.

Even Leslie seems to be enjoying it, the furrows from consternation and pain smoothing in favor of deepening smile lines. The oxycodone might be helping. His bulging white and red eyes glaze over. He gulps potatoes in great big swallows, same with the wine, and there's not enough of both for him, either, although I suspect he has different reasons.

"Told you," Zoe says through a mouthful of yams. Marshmallow fluff catches at the corners of her lips. "Pace yourself, though. You'll enjoy it more that way."

I slow down through the rest of the potatoes au gratin and roasted yams, altering between them every few bites to switch salty with sweet back to salty again, then sweet, then ending salty, so the last thing I taste is cheese cutting through the red wine. I cleanse it all out to ghosts with a deep drink from the water glass.

While I wait for everyone to finish their potatoes, I realize that a man across from me—not directly, but a few people to the left, one of the uncles or older cousins or whoever, I can't keep track of every who's who in the family—is masturbating.

With the table between us, if he were doing so discreetly, I wouldn't be able to tell. But he's quite blatantly stroking his dick. Impossible for even someone like me not to recognize, because I may be inexperienced, but after seven years of intermediate education, I don't think anyone's completely innocent. And now that I see what he's doing, I can hear it, too. His hand is in his pants, which limits some of his movement, but the sound is meaty and wet. And he's looking directly at me as he does it.

He's not the only one, either. That sound, that disgusting *sound*, like a dog licking his sheath or a buzzard swallowing roadkill—it's not just from him. There's another dissonant rhythm to the left of me. Not Duke—thank God—but someone down at the other table, with the elder and more well-regarded of the family. He's white-haired, long face with a patrician nose and defined cheekbones, almost gaunt. He's farther away, but the sound is less muffled, which means he has his dick whipped out of open trousers, despite his wife on one side of him and who I think is his son's wife on the other. He resembles neither Mother nor Father, but I think he's Mother's brother.

It doesn't matter who he is, nor does it make it better that he's not looking at me, because he's looking at someone and doesn't care who looks at him. And the one across from me, he *is* looking, and he feels no need to be subtle.

I squirm on the seat, but there's not enough room for that without getting too close to Zoe, too close to Duke. What I want more than anything at that moment—more than potatoes—is space. Space to breathe and not be seen. The scoop neck of my three-quarter-sleeve shirt seems too low now, though it doesn't show more than suggestion. Even if it didn't, that still doesn't earn me this naked regard that doesn't just rake but rips my clothes away by someone old enough to know better, because he was taught by Mother how to be polite.

I don't understand why she still laughs with Father, with their parents, when the sounds are loud enough for them to hear even over conversation—and after Mother got all out of joint over goddamn salt.

I adjust my shirt so the neckline is a little higher and to give the fit more folds to try to hide myself, but that only makes the uncle or older cousin grin, then lick his lips with a ruminative chew to the lower. He maintains his rhythm.

"Zoe…"

I keep doing this. I keep asking her to justify, and I keep accepting her justifications, holding on to her confirmations as though she's the arbiter, that if she's okay with this, it must be okay, even though I know *it is not okay.* None of this is okay, but everyone is just going along with it as though it's not just normal but truly part of the holiday spectacular, something they look forward to every year.

The potatoes don't make up for this, not by a long shot.

"Don't worry about him. It's harmless. Just ignore him. Hey, Uncle Conrad, you couldn't wait? Really?" Zoe threw up her arms at her uncle like a little sister annoyed at her sibling for playing a handheld under the table.

"It's not just him," I mutter. Now that I've seen one, then another, I notice other things. The guests not sitting next to the men being more obvious are noticing, too, now that starch isn't distracting them anymore.

A woman in a red dress fondles the man next to her. I think he's a guest, and he's clearly not minding. The orientation of her other arm suggests she's touching herself, too.

A woman in a button-up has undone three of her buttons, showing the pink lace of her bra.

Next to Layla, Matt strokes her fingers while he grips the front of his pants—not quite stroking but creating some stimulation on the bulge in his sweatpants. She's still just sitting there, staring at the table grain as though it shifts into visions.

I'd suspect an aphrodisiac in the potatoes, but some of us

are just uncomfortable, even if my vagina doesn't really know what kind of uncomfortable it's supposed to be, as confused as me. Not for the first time. My brain doesn't like it at all, any of it. The aftertaste of the potato course goes bitter sour in my mouth, like mold no longer concealed under cheese and marshmallow.

"Okay, okay, everybody…" Mother stands up again, still laughing from her conversation. Her cheeks are florid from the wine; it looks like a frown couldn't exist on her face if she tried. The only sign it still lives beneath the skin is a stipple-splatter of blood on her forehead and the stains on her sleeves that have gone brownish and stiff. "I know we're eager to move forward, but I'm a mother, and you know what Mother says: 'If you want dessert, you need to eat your vegetables first.' We're going to have our vegetable and salad course first, treat ourselves right on this day of overindulgence. Let's make sure to give our bodies what they need to make it all the way to midnight, my loves. That means carbs, yes, but we could use some good vitamins and minerals, too. Boys?"

The servers remove our used dinner plates and stack them neatly in the kitchen. Then they return with clean, white dinner plates with salad plates arranged on top. Nothing from Mother about the behavior of her family. Two guests are literally open-mouthed.

The mechanical clicking of a smartphone touchscreen, however, halts her conversation. She holds up her hand to quiet her side of the table, which makes the mechanical click all the louder.

The woman surreptitiously trying to call someone hasn't

the guile to make herself look innocent.

"No phones at the table." Mother turns her salad fork in her hand in steady rotation that stops her from making a fist.

"This isn't right. This isn't *right*." The uncomfortable woman across from me next to Uncle Conrad glances around the table as though expecting someone to join in her chorus, but even Leslie just rocks in place, staring at nothing in an eerily similar way to Layla. He shakes like someone jammed a live wire into his spine.

"You're absolutely right. This isn't right. We were explicitly clear about phones at the table. If there's anything that best exemplifies the deterioration of our civilization, it's screens—large and small—during mealtimes." Mother still doesn't stand. If anything, she leans on the table as though to prop herself up. I suppose she's had the same amount of wine as the rest of us—the world might tilt if I try to get up—but she should have better tolerance than me. She has a whole hutch dedicated to wine.

"Yeah, that's what's causing the decline of civilization, my phone and people asking for what they need and not the grown man over here literally jerking off while staring at a *child* across the table," the woman snaps. Even without cheerleaders, she gathers steam as she speaks. She knocks one of the server's arms away when they try to serve her a tossed Caesar salad. Even in her pretty, bohemian-patterned dress, she climbs off the bench with more ease than Leslie. "There are *children* here, and you…they…he… None of this is right. I'm calling the cops."

Matt uses Layla's chair and the table to vault over his

bench. His youth and athleticism allow him to maneuver between the servers to grab the phone out of the woman's hand. Without hesitation, he throws it to the ground. It's out of view, but the crunch of acorn shells underfoot suggests that multiple fractures on the screen have left it black, blank, broken.

"Children? There are no children down here," Mother says. "Everyone here is old enough to make their own decisions. If they were still children, they would be upstairs at the kids' table, watching kids' movies."

"You said your daughter and her roommate are in their first year of *college*," the woman replies. "Layla is only a year older, right? None of them should be seeing this. They shouldn't be seeing any of this."

"You didn't object when we served them alcohol. You didn't object when I set the record straight. And you didn't object when I cut off a man's hand and fed it to him. All these things you thought they were old enough to see. Who are you to make the decision about what's best? You're not a parent to any one of them."

Layla sighs sharply, or perhaps she gasps or scoffs. She gives nothing away in her expression when I look.

"And you think this is best for *your* children? Amputations and perverts and… God, you *are* sick. You're actually sick. Get *off* me!" The woman backhands a server, then knees Matt in the groin when he tries to stop her.

I consider becoming a cheerleader, but Zoe grips my upper arm so tightly I won't be surprised if bruises in the shape of her fingers rise there tomorrow. For the first time, she actually looks scared, but I don't think she's afraid of Conrad or Mother or even of what the woman will do as she darts into the kitchen, then toward the front of the house.

My heart punches off-beat against my lungs as the front door slams.

I want her to win. I want her to get out. She's a grown-up. It's her job to save us, even if we don't know enough to save ourselves. Even if Zoe, Duke, and Matt don't realize we need saving. I want her to bring red and blue lights flashing through the heavy drapes. I want this nightmare to fade, to wake up under clear darkness and cool sheets so I can turn over and reset. I want two plus two to equal four the way it's supposed to, and for actions to have proportionate consequences.

But I'm scared and small and my head swims. I can't knit together two sentences without being afraid of what Mother will do to me, with the salt from the last rainfall still cracking on my face like bad foundation. I just want this day to be over.

The grandfather clock in the corner loudly ticks each passing second that brings me closer to my goal. If I can just go unnoticed enough until the hands meet at the top, I can leave and never come back, never have to think about any of this again. So close, not even a whole day. I can do seven more hours. I can do seven more fucking hours if I have to, but I'd rather someone more grown up, someone bigger than me, make the decision. Save me. Save us.

Two servers drag the woman back in, one by her hair and the other by her arm. She swipes at them, but they're just out of reach. She screams as loudly as she can, as though she thinks someone in one of the other brick houses might hear, but they're all as tight and insulated as this one, and sound doesn't carry through air like it does through solids. If they didn't call the cops over Leslie's screams, they certainly aren't going to hear her.

My eyes sting. I'm crying before I realize I want to, although salad, bacon-cooked green beans, and candied carrots don't need that sort of seasoning.

Mother has the peeling knife again.

She washes it off at the sink as the servers arrange the woman back at the table with more ease than Leslie, although the server she struck has blood on his face from where his nose leaked, and the one whose balls she must have smashed like Matt's grimaces, hunched over not just to hold the woman down. She continues to fight, but the servers get a better grip on her thinner limbs, and their greater weight holds her down as much as their strength.

"The usual consequence for using a phone at the table is losing your thumbs, which makes it very difficult to text at my table again." Mother dries the knife off and holds it up to check for bloodstains she might have missed. "But I'm honestly more miffed by the simply awful things you had to say about my family. Really, Tawna, we're not monsters."

Zoe…

This time I know I don't say it. It won't make a difference. There's no stopping what's going to happen. And Uncle Conrad is stroking himself faster to me watching this unfold. He's pulled it out now. I can't see it, but I can't thank God for small favors. My imagination makes a worse picture than anything the man could show me. If there were something more than a wall behind me, maybe I would try to run, too, despite knowing I would fail.

"Wine is one thing. But not everyone here agreed to participate in *his* little fantasy." Tawna rears back and spits on Conrad instead of in the wine glass.

The wad gloops down his shirt, but if anything, he strokes himself faster, hips jerking up into his hand. He's grunting now, eyelids heavy. I want to look away, but looking at the woman puts him in my close periphery, clear enough to know everything that's happening.

"We didn't agree—*I* didn't agree—any more than we do on the bus or the subway or the station," Tawna says. "And I seriously doubt the man you maimed agreed to *that*. Maybe you're within the letter of the law on booze and sex, but what you did to him is bare-faced assault, several times over. Then you gave him prescription meds that aren't his. Don't stand there with your goddamn knife, acting all high and mighty on your moral high ground, when you're planning to maim me, too."

Mother stops behind Tawna and angles the blade into the interrogation lights over the table. I squint against the blinding, but I wouldn't blink if the action weren't involuntary.

"I believe I was clear about the rules," Mother says. "It's not a written contract but an implicit one: When you sit down at my table and eat my food, you agree to that contract. My daughter's roommate wasn't told all the details, so I gave her some leniency, but once I made things plain, you knew what would happen when you broke my rules. You agreed to this.

Just like you would agree to vomit if you deliberately took poison."

"That doesn't make it okay, or legal. Doesn't make it right," Tawna snaps, although her eyes are all white around like Leslie's were, and she tries to lean away from Mother as the servers lean her toward.

"Perhaps not legal. But I'm a mother and how I choose to punish those in my house is my domain, no one else's." She brings the point of the blade to Tawna's cheek.

When Tawna tries to buck back, she instead bucks into the blade, which digs its point into the flesh and draws a quick well of blood against the silver metal. Tawna cries out, but she's not screaming anymore. She looks up at Mother, around at the table, pleading silently for someone to stand for her, as she stood for us.

But we know Mother's rules.

"How?" she asks, tears thinning the blood and convincing it down her chin to disturb the pattern on her pretty dress. "How have you managed to get away with this for so long? How has no one stopped you? All these people here, all of them witnesses, all these years, how has no one stopped this?"

"Believe it or not, my dear, most feasts go without a hitch," Mother says, twisting the blade and raking cries from Tawna's throat. "We get the odd broken hand now and then when someone reaches for something they shouldn't, but we really don't have many of these little interruptions—sometimes none at all. The family knows how to comport themselves at my feasts. The children learn before they're allowed to sit at the grown-ups' table. Guests are granted some flexibility, especially those new to our family. What we offer far outweighs the dire consequences, because mistakes are easy enough to avoid. It's a simple social contract, Tawna, the same you have at tables all over this country and many outside of it.

"Perhaps you believe the consequences too dire, but really, how else will people learn to respect the boundaries that crumble around us every day? Children sass back at their parents while demanding expensive gifts. Elbows on the table. Take-out thrown on coffee tables for the wolves to descend. And at every restaurant we go to, yoga pants and faces buried in their little screens. It's unacceptable to everyone who remembers sit-down dinners with their family and wearing nice shoes to go out. Here, Tawna, we draw the lines and stick to them. That's the way a society is supposed to work. But rules don't mean we can't and shouldn't enjoy ourselves. This is a feast." Mother smiles as though explaining the good parts of dating with a daughter new to its world. "Good food, good mood, good company. That's not against the rules. The rules *protect* that. You, my dear, are the one who disturbed it."

Tawna pushes against the blade toward Mother, baring her teeth. "Do we look like we're having fun? You're sick. All of you are sick."

Mother bends down, smile unbroken. "I'm going to make you eat those words."

"No—"

Mother withdraws the knife and slaps Tawna across her bleeding check, splattering a handprint and smearing it along her face. "Oh, don't worry. I won't take your tongue. It's what caused all this trouble, but that would impede your ability to keep up with us for the rest of the day. Now, I can save the next course for your goodie bag, but vegetables won't warm up as well. Eat. Everyone, eat. You, too, Conrad. There will be more than enough time for that, and you're only human, no matter how many pills you take. Make it last."

Conrad swears under his breath—no trouble reading his lips—but he removes his hand from his dick and doesn't bother redoing his pants, just takes his fork in the same hand and eats his greens like a child scolded. I feel less seen, but it also makes a cardboard cutout out of me. I don't just feel dirty; despite the feast so far, I'm empty, hollow, a pleasing husk held in place not by a prop but by the person who brought me here.

"Come on, Sierra. Mother's candied carrots are the best, and she almost makes me like green beans." Zoe keeps her arm knotted with mine, but she can eat with her dominant hand, which leaves me only with my left.

I might as well be eating ranch-flavored paper with the Caesar salad—leafy greens have never been my favorite, and I fight not to gag—but green beans with bacon bring me back to earth, and the brown sugar and melted butter on the carrots sing. Even my salt doesn't hurt, and a shaking hand can still serve.

At knifepoint, Tawna reluctantly eats her vegetables, too. Leslie wolfs his down as though afraid the course is timed and he'll lose something else if he's last. Leslie lost a piece of himself already; Tawna has more to lose once she finishes.

But she can swirl around the smaller bacon bits in what's left of the candied sauce for only so long before she has to gather it on her fork and eat it, keenly aware that everyone around the tables watches, waits, in horror or anticipation. Without TV or phones, she's their entertainment, as is Mother as she eats her part of the meal standing over Tawna the whole time.

When Mother determines Tawna is finished, she hands her empty plate and Tawna's to one of the servers.

"You don't have to do this," Tawna says.

"Of course I don't *have* to do this. But if I don't, people will think they can run roughshod over my table, and that simply won't do."

Mother tucks Tawna's tousled hair behind her ear in a gesture as baleful as it is tender.

"Besides, I've been meaning to do this pork cheek recipe for a while. Granted, you won't yield much," she adds through Tawna's renewed struggles. "So you'll be the only one to enjoy the fruit of my spontaneous labors. You'll have to tell us whether you taste as good as you look. Sweetheart, if you keep flailing like this, it'll only be worse. There are all kinds of blood vessels and nerves here, and if I cut something I didn't intend to cut, you have only yourself to blame. If I were you, I'd stay perfectly still."

Mother sinks the skinning knife into Tawna's shallow face.

She carves rough harlequin diamonds from cheekbone to mandible on both sides. Halfway through the second cheek, she catches a vessel that spurts thick, bright red blood across the table. I jerk back when it splatters a line down my face.

Conrad grunts again, then abandons his fork to stroke himself through his climax. He paints a different sort of line in off-white across his own cheek.

I don't feel anything. My mind is on holiday. I barely register his comedown through the last strokes or the rest of Mother's work on Tawna, only that when I return, Zoe has cleaned the blood off my cheek, Tawna's face is a late Halloween mask, and she's sobbing and screaming but fighting to stay still. The right side of her face sags, which means Mother cut a nerve.

Tawna's teeth are uncanny white bone the same color as the bottom half of her scored cheekbones, and between her teeth, her tongue wriggles like a red eel.

It's worse. Worse than what happened to Leslie. Worse than what Conrad did. But then, Tawna made it farther and left her own marks. I bet she wishes she drew more than a burst capillary and swollen testicles.

Mother takes the cheeks—pathetic little cuts, because Tawna is a slender woman instead of a sow—to the stove and delicately skins them there on the plate.

"If I chose something more tender, I would be able to fry up something nice and fast for you, but you can't rush cheeks. Render fat for flavor, cook low and slow for tenderness. Under ordinary circumstances, I'd take the time to practice a new recipe, experiment with proportions, so I could offer you something truly extraordinary. But, my dear, you've forced me into improvisation, and your words weren't very nice, so you'll be more fortunate than I if what I give you is edible. And protein is absolutely necessary when your body is healing."

Mother dries the new cuts and salts and peppers them as she warms up a fresh pan. After coating the cheeks in flour, she throws a pat of butter in, then sears the meat.

She takes the cheeks off the pan to caramelize some leftover shallots. Apple cider vinegar and stock sizzles with the onions and leftover butter. She puts the cheeks back in the pan, lowers the temperature, covers the pan, then sets one of her dozen timers to an hour.

"For a proper serving, it would be twice that, but let's see where we are then." Mother kisses the top of Tawna's head. Tawna shudders as though dipped in an ice bucket. "George, I have a silk scarf I've been meaning to donate. You know the one."

"The pink one with the flowers." After finishing his red wine, he spits in the glass to signal the rest of us to do the same as he leaves the table for their bedroom again.

I barely manage to gather enough saliva, but it's something, and I pass it along. I have Zoe's glass in front of my setting again.

Father returns with a soft pink scarf draped over his arm. Great big red watercolor poppies mask the bloom of bloodstains as Mother winds it around Tawna's face and head. No pain meds this time. No cauterization, either, just free flow of facial blood. Silk is a natural, breathable fiber, and Mother doesn't tie it tightly, but I worry Tawna's mucusy sobs mean she's not getting enough air—through nose, mouth, or cheeks—and that absorption isn't ideal to slow her bleeding.

And I wonder whether that would be best.

"Good girl," Mother murmurs into the cocoon. Tawna twitches as though bitten by a spider. "Don't go anywhere. As long as this is on, you're exempt from consumption, but I'm afraid you still have to stay."

On the way back to her throne, Mother checks over the table to make sure that all the salad plates have been cleaned off and cleared from the dinner plates.

"Oh, excellent, everyone. In case you needed something to justify the rest of our bacchanal, remember your salad plate with fondness. We return now to our usual dissolute decadence."

I laugh only because everyone else laughs. I don't have to hear how little my laugh actually sounds like one.

"Okay, while we retrieve the trays from the other fridge, why don't we play a little musical chairs without changing spots? Both wine glasses move five places to the left. Those next to our injured, please help them with their glasses. I'll be right back."

"This is the fun part," Zoe whispers, aiming for my ear, but the cool breeze of her breath disturbs the little hairs on the back of my neck, which starts a chain reaction along my scalp.

Maybe I'm drunk. I wouldn't know. If this numb confusion is what drunk is, I think I'll take it over clarity. The last thing I need is for the edges of this world to sharpen.

Raucous cheers rise from the family as the first server enters the room with a baking pan full of little lidded plastic cups filled with brightly colored gelatin.

Thanksgiving dinner with a suburban family cult is not where I thought I'd have my first Jell-O shot.

Duke and Matt both have deafening claps. I cover my ears until they stop. The servers put five plastic containers on everyone's plate, as well as a toothpick. I don't know how Jell-O shots work, so I just wait to see what the toothpick is for, because it's certainly not for gelatin getting stuck between our teeth.

"What's in them?" I ask Zoe. It's not just Jell-O, or else people wouldn't get so excited.

"The pink ones are homemade strawberry champagne. The rest are traditional Jell-O with whipped cream vodka. They're so good, Sierra." She brings me closer, shifting from holding my arm to practically an embrace as she laughs against my neck. "They'll massage right through all this tension still left after the wine."

"I'm not sure that's a good idea." I want to forget what's going on around me, but I also really shouldn't look away from what no one's stopping, including me—even though I shouldn't have to. Because I wouldn't have thought that 'don't masturbate at the table' and 'don't disarticulate a limb or mutilate a face' should have to be said, and yet…

"It makes it easier," Zoe says. "It makes everything easier."

This bewilders me on top of everything else, because Zoe is usually as much of a stickler for no alcohol in the dorm room as I am. She never comes home drunk, as far as I can tell, and we only ever have orange juice and soda in the fridge.

I wipe at my face, brushing away the tears. "Is Thanksgiving dinner supposed to be this hard?"

"Some of us are," Duke mutters behind me.

"It's okay. Everything's okay, I promise." Zoe reaches around me to take Duke's hand and guide it to my leg, then slide it over my inner thigh.

I jump, my wide-eyed stare fixed on Zoe, stunned silent again.

Mother opens her strawberry champagne gelatin and raises it like her wine glasses. "I think the best kinds of food and drink stimulate all the senses. We associate a home-cooked meal with comfort, spice with soul. This little palate cleanser"—she shakes the cup to make the shot jiggle—"will give us a chance to enjoy what good food and good company do for our bodies, in all kinds of ways. While we take a short break from food, let's work up an appetite, shall we? The shots are mandatory; the rest of our extracurricular course is not. But if you feel any hesitation, ask yourself if it's yours—or from out there. I think we've established we don't give a flying figgy pudding what people out there think."

She loosens the gelatin from the cup with the toothpick—*so that's how it works*—then throws her head back to suck the strawberry champagne down. Everyone drinks the strawberry champagne with her first, except Tawna, the only one without shots on her plate. She whimpers, muffled, and clings to the table—faceless as a mannequin, the dips of her eye sockets and cheek sockets eerier without definition.

Zoe takes her shot, then picks up mine when I don't go for it immediately with the rest. She slides the toothpick into the container and swirls it around the edge with distracting deliberation. She's doing it on purpose; I'm tempted to let her. I'm tempted by several things, all of which are much more pleasant than whatever the hell else is going on.

She brings the container to my lips and winks. "This isn't even the hard stuff."

In all my years of flooding teenage hormones, sometimes too intense as I grew into the feelings, I can't remember being as uncomfortably aroused as this—maybe because it's never been real before. This isn't the kind of thing I think is supposed to happen to people, but neither is everything else, so why should this be any different?

I swallow the strawberry champagne all at once, the nostalgic texture of gelatin smooth and easy. When I stretch out my tongue to gather what didn't come loose, Zoe whimpers like a kitten. She barely waits to draw the container away before her mouth is on mine.

If I could stop kissing her back, I'd tell her she didn't have to invite me to her fucked-up family feast for us to kiss over Jell-O shots. Hell, I wouldn't have been mad if she'd also invited her cousin Duke. I'm not mad as he runs an unexpectedly hot tongue over my neck and strokes over my inner thigh with bold confidence that tells me he's done this before. I don't want to know who with, and I don't want to know if it was at one of these feasts. I don't care.

I draw his hand further up my thigh to where I'm so turned on it hurts, and I wind my fingers through Zoe's curly hair, tasting strawberry champagne until she grabs one of the shots from her plate and brings it to our noses to entice me away.

Cherry Jell-O with whipped cream vodka. I grab mine, open it up, squeeze the edges to loosen the gelatin, then suck it down.

"Oh, fuck me," Duke groans against my shoulder. He straddles the bench to press himself closer, his cock insistent and unabashedly physical against my side, but fortunately still within his pants. I don't think I could… I don't know whether I'm… I moan as he finds a place just below the angle of my jaw that makes me tingle everywhere—and a few places in particular, one of which he strokes with no finesse or focus, but it's new and amazing to have anything there at all that isn't mine alone.

Then Zoe's guiding my face back down and kissing me again. This time we taste of maraschino cherries.

I close my eyes so I can't see what's going on, but I can only try not to hear, and I fail.

When Duke and Zoe are on either side of my neck, my eyelids flutter, and morbid, disgusting curiosity compels me to look, because whether stone or salt or highway fatality, we always look, and what we don't see, our imagination fills in the blanks even more luridly.

I'm fortunate that all the adults are behind me. I don't know whether my unfortunately unfragile mind would be able to handle watching Mother and Father together, or their parents, or any of the other elders at their end.

All I really see from my angle is Matt with Layla. He's sitting on her lap. She barely moves. Just her hand in his lap, mechanically going through the motions of jerking him off. He doesn't seem to mind the mechanics. He's groaning like she's the best thing he's ever had in his life. Maybe this is his first time, like me; or maybe, like me, he's just young. But I don't like Layla's blue-glass-marble eyes, or that the only signs of life in them are when she glances furtively up the table, then looks away again, then back, then away—dying and dead in turns.

I reach behind me and feel my way up Duke's pants until I find his cock through the fabric. He swears, his breath scorching against my neck, blowing down the back of my shirt.

I have my own curiosity and just enough wine and bubbling champagne and pleasure to satisfy it. I've never seen anything except in pictures, illustrated and secretive peeks online when I'm not looking over my shoulder to make sure no one can see me looking. What I remember in two dimensions doesn't prepare me for what I touch in three, smaller and bigger than I expect all at the same time. I blindly explore until I manage a good grip through the sweatpants and he's grunting like Conrad, which makes me shake in a way that has nothing to do with Zoe's cool fingers creeping up the front of my shirt. But I don't stop, because this, at least, is something I choose.

He's damp against my side now, panting fever against my skin as he rubs my back in gratitude.

We fumble for the next shot—key lime.

In the corner of my eye, Tawna turns her featureless face to the light, with muffled cries that could be confused for pleasure instead of pain from the silk layers between face and clean air. I'm not so tipsy that I believe she wants the shoulder of her dress pulled down to expose her small breast with more clarity than her face. A large hand squeezes her too hard, then twists her nipple to keep it flushed brown and wrinkled tight and hard.

I swallow my shot, then climb onto my knees on the bench to crawl over Zoe. She reads me with blown pupils to the edge of her unholy pale and pulls me down to straddle her. We balance each other as we ride, hands and fingers in new electric places while my head spins and dips like an aquatic animal through the haze of booze. If I can't shut my ears, at least I can close my eyes or see nothing but Zoe's beautiful face framed by the curtain of my hair.

I think Duke strokes himself off again at the sight of us. Matt might, too. So might others at the table, but if I'm not sure, it might as well not be real. When Zoe comes, we take another shot—lemon. With a pucker in the back of our mouths, she licks my tongue through my orgasm, which shakes me apart and puts me back together before I spill to the floor in single cells. We don't stop there, but we do take the last shot—watermelon.

When we emerge from the seaweed knot of sweat-locked hair, we're tangled at the legs, wet stains on our thighs, shirts and bras in disarray, and Zoe has a stupid-drunk smile dazzling half her face, the other half taken up by eyes. If I let her go, I might topple over to the side.

"Don't worry, we're going to eat more. That and water should help." She's slurring, which is an improvement on me. I was already having trouble putting a thought through the needle's eye.

"Why didn't—" I speak through a wet-dry mouthful of molasses. "Why didn't we...before?"

"I wanted it to be special." She combs through my hair— easier to tend the mess in mine than hers, which coronas her head from all the ways I held it in my fists.

I tug on my shirt, then try to adjust my bra back in place. That's the wrong order. I pull up my shirt to put my boobs back in their respective cups, then pull the shirt back down to hide the stains on my leggings. "I need to pee. I can go pee, can't I?"

She giggles, but she helps as well as she can to steady me as

I climb off. Duke helps, too, although he's rested his head on the table. His gaze follows me as I round Layla, who is alone again and gray as ash. If she weren't blinking, I would assume she had a fatal heart attack or stroke, despite her age.

Servers hand out moist towelettes like we had a sticky dessert, but I wave them away and try to navigate a straight-ish line through the kitchen to the front of the house. It's not just the dampness in my underwear or the lingering heaviness of arousal tingling in my lower abdomen and all the places she touched me that make me think I need to pee. Alcohol might be a culprit, too, the pressure on my bladder too urgent too quickly. Fortunately, no one's in the powder room, and I close the door, lock it, then collapse back on the toilet.

I can still hear everyone, but it's as though they're on the other side of the street. The quiet on this side of the house buzzes in my ears. I can't keep my eyes open.

Between vodka, endorphins, and oxytocin—and the fact that my purse was taken off my shoulder at some point, so I can't check my phone for the time, if they would even let me do that—I can't tell how long I'm in the bathroom once I scrabble back to semi-consciousness and clean myself off. I wash my hands, then splash some water on my face and drink coolness from the faucet before pushing myself up and facing my reflection.

I'm still me, though wilted. My tongue's dyed several different colors. I have pepper in my teeth, but not anywhere that anyone would have been able to easily see unless I smiled too wide. I pick at the pepper with my nail, then wash my hands again.

I'm given a few seconds' warning as the world tilts one way, then the other, with my stomach taking the opposite direction each time, sloshing everything I've eaten that hasn't passed through into my intestines. I fall to my knees and manage to get most of the multi-colored, sour, stinging vomit into the bowl, with a few spatters along the back.

"Sierra, are you okay?" Zoe sounds like she's right behind me. She must have her mouth against the door.

"Yeah. Give me a minute."

Vomiting doesn't sober me up, but the world's tilt returns to its usual axis. I find anti-bacterial spray and clean what doesn't flush, wash my hands again, then use the complimentary hand lotion, because I still smell vomit in the back of my nose like the need to cry.

When I open the door, Zoe's there, but so is Mother. She looks the same as she did before the shot palate cleanser rather than disheveled like her daughter. I consider it a small favor. She's not frowning, but she's searching. I check to make sure I've wiped all my mouth. Then I realize what she isn't asking, and I drop my arm with a sharp scoff.

"I didn't do it on purpose," I say. "I don't do that. I don't even know how to. I just don't drink. I've never had to hold my liquor before."

"She really doesn't drink, Mother," Zoe interjects. "There's been a lot of new things today. I might have pushed too hard. You sure you're okay, Sierra?"

"I feel a little better." The downside to expelling most of the Jell-O shots, even if the alcohol already permeated my blood, is that some of the fuzziness is gone. Reality creeps in like dusk through the front door windows.

Mother offers me a new shot, this time a little plastic measuring cup of Pepto Bismol. I take it gladly, although the fake flavor is chalky and sickly sweet as I swallow.

"Can you eat?" she asks.

She means, *Have I the stomach for it?* The answer is no, but short of projectile vomiting in a way I can attribute to violent food poisoning, what choice do I have? And honestly, food poisoning could be the biggest insult of all, so I pray the queasiness lifts now that my stomach expelled the excess.

I try not to glance at the front door. "I'm drunk, not sick. I think I'll be all right." Two truths and a lie, like being polite is a game.

As Mother takes the little, pink-stained cup, she strokes my cheek with tenderness I associate with my own mom, inspiring an even worse pang of homesickness I almost mistake for needing to throw up again. She then presses cool fingers to my forehead.

"You're a little flushed, but that's to be expected. You don't have a fever. Do you need some orange juice or ginger ale? You aren't the first to feel a little sick at one of these. Those Jell-O shots do sneak up on you if you're not used to them."

"Is it okay if I just open my sparkling juice? I'm probably the only one who wants it anyway."

Mother chuckles a little. "Of course. Let me get you a separate glass for that, so it doesn't mix with water or wine."

She heads into the kitchen again, leaving me alone with Zoe in the hall that connects the kitchen and foyer, the stairs looming behind me.

"You sure you're okay? It wasn't me, was it?" Zoe asks, suddenly shy. Maybe she's the opposite of average—as she is in so many ways—and gets more reserved with alcohol instead of less. Spirits certainly strip away the layers between the wall of masks and the chest of insecurities once the action is done and the equal and opposite reaction comes hurtling toward you.

"No, I'm serious. I think it was the wine with the vodka chasers," I reply. "I'd say I should pace myself, but I don't really get to choose how I do that here, do I?"

"At least home's a safe place to test those limits."

She mistakes the disbelief in my eyes with preoccupation with her lips, but even after throwing up then drinking water and Pepto Bismol, she's still nice to kiss, especially now that no one can make it part of their course when I didn't bring that dish for them.

Zoe pushes me lightly until I hit the wall, but she's unhurried and un-insistent, fighting a smile the whole time.

I grip her shoulders, consider pulling her closer again, but I push her back instead. "We could have done this any other time. We could have done this last night. We can do it tomorrow night. What if I just left now? I think I can eat, but I probably shouldn't."

Zoe shakes her head in confusion. "I don't understand. I thought you liked it. I thought you liked me."

"I do. That's not what I'm saying. But why did it have to be *here*? Why not when we were watching *Moulin Rouge!* or *The Mummy* or something? In private."

"Are you ashamed? Because I thought, since you aren't religious, you wouldn't have a problem with—"

"I don't have a problem with being with a girl. *This*"—I gesture between the two of us—"isn't the problem. But why? Why did you have to make this happen at the same time as everything else? Why did we have to do that in front of everyone, your parents, your siblings, your cousins, perfect strangers? Your Uncle Conrad wasn't the only one jerking off to us, and I didn't agree to that. I'm drunk. You know I'm drunk. I've had more today than in two years at family gatherings. Why couldn't it have just been you and me and locks on the door, pizza in the microwave, snack cakes in the drawer? Why did you have to do it *now*, when you had to clean smeared blood off my face and I had to remember your Uncle Conrad coming because that woman bled on me? Goddammit, Zoe!" My whisper grates harsh lines in my throat as I try not to call too much attention to me in this moment of finally speaking freely, the way I've always done with her.

"We look forward to this every year," she says slowly, still staring as though I'm speaking in tongues, as though she's never met me before. "It's freeing. We wipe everything people tell us on the outside away from our shoes on the welcome mat. I wanted you to meet my family. I wanted you to meet Mother and Father. I wanted you to spend more time with other people. I wanted you to relax and have a good time. I didn't want you overthinking it. I thought if we could have the shots and everyone else was doing it, enjoying it, enjoying you as much as I do, you'd have just as special of a time as us."

She isn't the only one seeing a stranger. It isn't that she's saying things that don't match what I know of her. On the contrary, this sounds like just the sort of thing she'd say—about a party on another floor of our dorm, with seniors instead of fish, or at a sorority or fraternity event, even if she was unsure if she wanted to pledge.

But what about me makes her think I wanted my first kiss, my first drunken make-out session, my first over-the-clothes fuck, in front of her family? What makes her think I wanted all those things to happen for the first time while a man digests his missing hand and cradles the stump? What makes her think I wanted those things to happen for the first time while a woman drowns in her own blood and tears, her every word exposed? Or that I wanted to be not tipsy, not buzzed, but drunk enough to vomit afterward? Or that I wanted to be shouted at for salt then cheered for showing off to her family how many times I can get their daughter off while we're dampened with booze? I was drunk enough to do it, but I'm not drunk enough to not regret or for my mostly empty stomach to not roil with what I was willing to roll with.

I don't know how to tell her that without hurting her feelings more than I already have. Besides, Mother returns with a tall water glass of my sparkling juice on ice. Condensation chills my palm when she passes it to me.

"Next course is soon," she says to both of us, but mostly to Zoe. I don't know how much she's heard. I have to assume everything. It's better in general to assume that moms know everything—especially Mother, who's just looking for a reason with me, one way or another.

A timer goes off.

"I need to prepare the cheeks. Five minutes, girls." Mother backs into the kitchen again.

"The door's right there," I whisper. "I won't call the cops. I won't call anyone. We'll forget this ever happened—just a day-drinking dream. You can bring my purse home. You can tell them I threw up again and I'm still not feeling well. I can't go back in there. I can't stand them seeing me when they've seen so much more. I never would have…" I take a breath, take a drink. I don't worry that Mother spiked the juice. If she poisons me, I can't finish her feast. "Please, Zoe. Thank your family for their unique hospitality, but I can't do this."

"It's rude to leave halfway through a dinner, especially when you just threw up the first half," Zoe hisses back at me, as though I'm embarrassing her, an unexpected burden to carry over a finish line. "What are you going to do to get home without your phone? Walk? Don't be ridiculous. Look, I know you're self-conscious, but I promise other people were doing much more. Most of them were probably just as wrapped up in each other as we were. They didn't see anything. And the rest of them don't matter. They *don't matter*, Sierra. I'm sorry you had more alcohol than you could handle, but it's just wine from here on out, interspersed with plenty of food. The shots were just for fun. We'll save the rest of *this* for tonight. For that privacy you want. But you can't leave yet. Please don't. Come on. Come on."

She gently pulls on my hand. We're almost two arms outstretched before I let her drag me back into the kitchen, where Mother arranges a small plate of much diminished cheeks in their sauce. It's not restaurant-quality presentation, but it looks clean, intentional—a plated gift. A sprinkle of diced parsley stems ties the bow.

"I'm sorry I threw up," I murmur. I don't even know what I'm supposed to say to a normal family when things like this happen. But if there's one thing I know, it's that I don't want to offend an already suspicious Mother.

She's calmer, though, now that I'm back in the kitchen, in her domain rather than in view of the front door. "It's no trouble at all. As long as it wasn't intentional, no harm, no foul. Drink up, dear. It'll help settle your stomach."

"Thanks." My voice is weak, especially as Mother takes the cooked cheeks to the table and sets it on Tawna's dinner plate with pride.

Zoe leads me back around to the younger side of the table. Duke grins up at me, more or less put back together, apart from the stains, but there are stains all over the table. Some people didn't even bother to clean up the semen on themselves and each other. I drink half of my sparkling juice and hope it partners with the Pepto Bismol to convince what's left in my stomach to remain there.

"Can I wipe this—" I indicate my plate, which has a splatter of watery seed across the white. I can't believe I have to ask.

"It's just a little extra salt and protein," Zoe says. "It's not technically something that Mother serves, but it's part of the last course. Like sharing our glasses."

"This is more than swapping spit, Zoe."

"We only use our plate for two courses at a time. Given how everyone shares, no one would hurt themselves to hurt us.

Besides, at least a quarter of the stomachs in here already have some inside them. It's not going to hurt anything."

I can't say what I want to say. I can't tell her that's dangerous and fucking disgusting. I can't tell her that there's not enough Pepto or carbonation to take the taste of bile away if it keeps bubbling up to the back of my throat. Because to say so would be to insult the course, even if Mother didn't prepare it.

Conrad partially unbuttoned his shirt and wears his cum proudly so that I have to see it every time I look across the table. I don't have the luxury of turning away again now that everyone's returned to their place and awaits the next course.

Almost everyone. The place next to Leslie is empty, and he's clutching his leg as he twitches through an impending seizure from blood loss.

No, that's not right. He's only losing seepage through the sear. His face is bloodless, but he's not seizing. The barking moans aren't from pain or shock, and the place next to him isn't empty. He jerks up into Phillipa's urgent, eager mouth, his fingers not on his leg but in her hair.

She's the one who brought him here. Maybe this is where he thought it would go by the end of the night. Maybe he even knew it would be in front of everyone. Maybe that excited him. Bet he didn't know he'd only be able to hold her down with one hand when it finally happened.

I can imagine her whispering in his ear when the course began that there was no reason why they couldn't still do it. The pain meds could have taken enough of the edge off and, mixed with alcohol, left him vulnerable to the kind of suggestion that wouldn't have him thinking twice under normal circumstances. I can't speak to his logic. Or maybe that's the problem right there—that I expect logic from a man getting sucked off by a beautiful woman, regardless of the circumstances. I'm hardly one to throw stones. I was tipsy, not drunk, when the last course started.

I hear endorphins from orgasm help with pain management.

I can't look away while it's happening. I've never seen a real orgasm face, not so clearly and not from a man. It's horrifying—the fact that he has an orgasm face, not the orgasm face itself. As far as how it looks, it's not so far from if a hammer had slammed into his kneecap—just a different stimulation that causes it.

And because I can't look away, I can't ignore Conrad's reaction to my reaction.

He isn't the only one who sees that I'm watching. Duke sneaks his hand over my thigh again. The whole zone between my legs may still be confused as hell, but I'm not. I try not to be mean as I take his hand and put it back in his lap.

Zoe leans back to mouth something at him. I hope she's telling him not to take it personally. Because he was raised in this like Zoe, he seems to be completely oblivious to the fact that *none of this is okay*, even if I lost myself in the moment. A very long moment. I didn't realize it was already almost six.

Roughly six hours left until they let us leave.

If they let you leave.

In fact, there's no real reason they have to, is there? Unless they have assurances, more than spoken, that we keep silent about this whole thing. Plenty of people married in.

I wonder if anyone in the family is ordained.

Now that my head is a little clearer, I understand I need to start considering what I'm willing to do to get out of here. Because, given that Tawna is screaming as Mother unwinds the scarf cocoon, no grown-up is going to save us.

The first layer of silk sticks to her face from the dried blood. Her dress is back to where it should be, but her lips are even paler than Leslie's, and blood drips again when Mother disturbs the cruor. From the way the bloodstains on the silk spread the blood around, Tawna's face looks like she used dark red lipstick to paint everything beneath her eyes—no more or less of a horror show than before the silk cocoon, but different.

"Please, let me go." Her teeth click like pearls in velvet. I'm distracted by the shape of her words in the holes. Without the walls of her oral cathedral, air blows through like wind through an organ. Some of the nerves and muscles that control the mandible have been cut, making it difficult for her to enunciate or even completely close her teeth. "Don't make me do this. Let me go. I won't do anything. I promise. I need a hospital."

"Harold over there is a surgeon. Always good to have at least one of those in the family," Mother says, rearranging Tawna's hair into something more kempt. "Not a cosmetic surgeon, but he can take care of injuries like this. After the feast, he'll take a look at your face and Leslie's hand."

"We can't wait that long. We won't last 'til midnight. Infection…"

"You should have thought of that before. Harold has antibiotics, but he's on his day off, not even on call. This is his time, not yours. Now, your special treat finished cooking and smells amazing, if I do say so myself. I know it hurts, but you should still be able to chew and swallow without leaking much more than gravy. Then we should be able to move on to the next course."

"I'm not… I'm not going to do that." Tawna's sobbing again, looking at the diminished pieces of her face in their apple cider vinegar gravy puddle. "I can't fucking do that, you fucking witch."

"Those are two different statements, but the answer to both of them is the same. You will. I'm serving this to you; therefore, you will eat it. Otherwise, there are other parts of you that would be more generous to this table. These are just two small swallows. Such a small thing in comparison to what Les ate. At the very least, you'll be delicious."

Mother hands Tawna a fork.

Tawna's elegant hand trembles like the earth as she hovers the fork over the plate. She stabs the tines into the meat, shuddering. Wet sobs bubble blood and saliva through the holes. She puts the bite in her mouth, clenching her eyes shut at the new flood of tears.

Then she turns her head and spits the cheek at Mother. Gravy spews over Mother's face.

Mother closes her eyes in reflex. The sad piece of meat rolls like a pebble down Mother's shirt onto the floor. When she opens them again, her pale eyes are as dead as her daughter Layla's, but I doubt for the same reasons.

Mother wipes her face with her fingers, gathering gravy, before grabbing Tawna by the neck. She squeezes so hard that Tawna coughs and gags, mouth open for Mother to smear the gravy on Tawna's tongue, then slam her jaw closed, severing the tip of her tongue in the process.

Now that Tawna proves her lesson unlearned, the servers grab her in the same hold in which they pinioned Leslie.

Mother takes that piece of freshly severed tongue, soaked in the new blood pouring from Tawna's mouth, and sets it on the plate. She bends under the table to retrieve the spat cheek, now just an unadorned piece of meat. She puts it next to the sauced cheek and tongue.

"Child, it's not a question of whether you eat it. It's how tasty it is when you do. Now, I'm a good host. I cleaned the floors before everyone came. But all our feet have been on this floor today, so I can't promise the meat itself is clean, which may only be appropriate for such a filthy mouth. We have a surgeon in the house, but we also have a dentist in Margaret, which means we have spare cheek retractors and bite blocks. You have three choices here: You can chew, you can swallow, or you can choke. We're not moving on to the next course until you've had your treat, and that's going to make all the other guests and the family mad, because they've worked up another appetite by now. They'll have neither wine nor fowl while you're acting like an intransigent toddler. Mine might not be the only retribution you suffer. Now, turn the other cheek, eat your words, and have some dignity."

Tawna lifts her fork again and stabs the cheek that fell on the floor, then puts it in her mouthful of blood. This time, we watch the bovine rumination, crushing the meat into something as suitable to swallow as she can amid the pain and without the muscles to use her mandible properly. After a moment's hesitation, she takes the other cheek and does the same. Some gravy slips out, but Mother dabs at the wound edges and doesn't make her eat the excess, since she doesn't lose that part on purpose.

"All of it, my dear."

Tawna picks up the piece of her tongue between her nails and drops it into her mouth, throwing her head back like taking a pill. When she drinks some water to help her swallow, that trickles from her mouth stained red as well, and Mother tends to her once again.

"Good girl. Now we can continue, and so can you. You'll need the protein, just like your rude friend down the table, and I imagine you won't regret the wine, although you'll have to hold your head back more, won't you?" Mother pats Tawna's hair like she's an obedient pet, then returns to the head of the table as the servers fill bread baskets with the rolls that remain, warmed in a low-temperature oven.

They go by again with the bread assortment and white wine. This time, everyone only takes one, just in case. I choose a Hawaiian roll instead of a croissant, because it seems sufficiently both bland and flavorsome enough to settle my queasiness. I eat slowly, with little bites, and I alternate between wine and sparkling juice. Lulled conversations louden to friendly arguments. Zoe tries to include me in a discussion about Duke's math issues, but without the pages in front of me, I'm not much help and not particularly talkative, so she rubs my back as though the issue is just the nausea and talks around me with Duke, sometimes Matt behind her.

After so many filling things to eat, they're not in as much of a hurry through the courses. And I'm not very hungry anymore, either, despite emptying some of that more substantial fare.

I take advantage of their patience to run through my limited options. It doesn't help that Tawna is almost right in front of me every time I consider my exits and the location of sharp or hot implements. My place at the table puts me in a good position to run through the kitchen, which has weapons, and to the front door for escape, but Tawna had an even better position. She's a blood-soaked example that I only get one shot.

I don't know the blueprint of the back of the house. I know the main bedroom is reached through the hallway off the den. I know there's a full bath on the other side of the door to the right of that hallway entrance. I don't know where the left door leads, but it looks like it's to a linen or storage closet, not outside. There's another door tucked to the left of the den entertainment system, behind Mother, which might lead to the garage but might also lead to another room. The main suite might or might not have a door to the backyard. The lower half of the windows have mesh screens—not impossible to get through, especially with something sharp, but that requires extra time I probably won't have.

My best bet is getting out the front door and hoping that, among doctors, dentists, and school athletes, the family doesn't have a track medalist or marathoner.

That gets me out, but then I have to run back to the university, where I live with the person who brought me here in the first place and for whom my feelings are mixed in a goddamn food processor. Because I know she didn't bring me here to get hurt, but she brought me here knowing I might, and she certainly didn't prepare me so I wouldn't. Thinking about kissing her again makes my head swim like the wine, but thinking about kissing her after this whole thing is done also makes me sick, and I don't know if I'll ever be able to untangle those feelings—Zoe's beautiful, big, piercing pale eyes and Tawna's bloody terror, Duke's hand on my leg, and higher, and Leslie's hand twitching into his stomach.

Racing thoughts in a quiet body, I don't realize how tired I am—from sugar, starch, and wine, from the adrenaline crash, from feeling sick, from being scared—until Zoe shakes me awake.

She giggles when I jolt upright from my plate as though I missed a morning class exam. "Good morning, angel. Don't worry. You weren't snoring. Some drool, but no snoring. You only have a little more to eat, but the next two courses are that quintessential American Thanksgiving you've been waiting for."

Everyone else is finished, but no one's glaring, so I quickly eat what's left of my bread and wash it down with the rest of the wine. As soon as I finish, though, everyone spits into their wine glasses, like they were waiting all along.

Duke doesn't seem to care any more than Zoe did that I threw up less than an hour ago.

While the servers bring out more red wine for everyone,

Mother and Father roll a large butcher block island—one that isn't still bloody from the amputation—into the center of the kitchen. Mother opens one of the ovens and pulls out a beautifully golden-brown turkey surrounded by caramelized roasted apples. The casserole dishes below hold the dressing. Father pours simmering gravy into gravy boats. One of the servers carries homemade cranberry sauce.

Mother carves the turkey; Father serves what she cuts. The servers dish out the mushroom, sausage, and sage dressing and the cranberry sauce, then follow the meat with gravy for the turkey, dressing, or both. We have an option for half an apple, which I accept, if just to make the course last longer, which gives me time to think and brings us closer to the end.

Maybe everything doesn't actually stop at the stroke of midnight regardless whether we finish. Maybe midnight is just an approximation of when we'll finish. But it's a reference point either way.

I don't like the turkey. Everyone has a piece each of white meat and dark. The dark meat is better, but I can't understand why anyone would choose turkey when they could have chicken or ham, which carry much more flavor. I'm grateful for gravy—the same gravy as on the mashed potatoes and still good, although it could use more salt and I'm too focused on the problem to cry for it. The dressing, too, is delicious. I'd have another serving of that instead of the cranberry sauce, which is both too tart and too sweet, although drinking wine with it gives it a more tolerable fruity taste.

The roasted apple is like a dessert— a self-contained apple pie sans crust—and for me, it's even better than the dressing.

By the end of the first quintessential American Thanksgiving dinner course, which is underwhelming in comparison to the potatoes, I'm no closer to figuring out how to get out of this place. I'm also near tears again, maybe because I'm still tired and because Tawna streams tears of her own as she struggles to eat what's been put in front of her.

Once the turkey has been broken down to its edible parts and the architecture of its bones—bones then broken down more and stored in the plastic container with what's left of the buffalo chicken wings—Mother sets the leftover turkey aside, sliced for sandwiches and cubed for soups, in its own plastic containers. Then she pulls three more casserole dishes out of another oven.

Spit into the wine glass, pass, more red wine.

I'm starting to feel a little tipsy again, but the servers bring around the casserole dishes, these filled with actual casseroles: cheesy broccoli rice casserole, green bean casserole, and squash casserole. All look directly out of a seventies recipe book. I suppose they endure for a reason, but I choke down the unpleasant textures of the green bean and squash casseroles and try my hardest not to insult the chef by audibly gagging. I finish all three of my drinks to help me swallow.

The broccoli rice casserole more than makes up for the other two, which is a pleasant surprise, since I usually don't like broccoli, either.

By the end of a course that weighs heavy in an uncertain stomach, I'm still right where I started—no escape, no options without a high probability of failure and, thus, dismemberment.

Duke nudges me with his elbow. Maybe Zoe taught him to do that, or vice versa. He nods toward Leslie, who's swaying in circles on the bench. His face is gray, sockets shaded, and his breathing is shallow and fast.

All the grown-ups on his side of the table watch him, too, as though he's a serpent and they the prey.

But that's backward, isn't it? They're ravening and ravenous, chewing, chewing, chewing, biting with incisor, tearing with canine, crushing with molar, speaking and swallowing with the same long, wet muscle. Too many pale eyes. And in spite of all they've eaten, they're still hungry, color leached from his face into theirs, high on cheeks Tawna no longer has but for bone. They lock arms and rest their heads against shoulders like lovers at a romantic look-out, staring at stars. I'm one of them, with Zoe's arm in mine, both of us watching this macabre drive-in, waiting for the moment we all know will come.

Leslie's eyes roll back, until they seem all bloodshot white but for the sliver of brown under his eyelids. He falls, almost in slow motion until momentum and gravity take hold when the servers do not. His head hits the hardwood floor before his bottom half slides off the bench to join him in an undignified heap.

I climb off the bench to crouch under the table.

His pants are open, his cock a soft, spent slug uncovered from after Phillipa finished with him. In spite of his uncomfortable position, he's still breathing—shallow, slow. Alive, although I don't know for how long.

I'm not sure why he's the first to fall when he ostensibly

lost less blood than Tawna, who's inconsolable because she can't keep it all in her mouth—pieces and juices and mucus and gravy coating the front of her dress like undigested vomit—and because they never gave her one of the pills they gave Les. Despite her misery, it's impossible not to see her skull grinning with the perpetual smile they always tell us to have.

Expose your bones to us. It'll make you feel better and improve our view.

"Papa, Conrad, can you take Les into the other room?" Mother waves her spoon of green bean casserole at the tangled lump of body. "He appears unable to finish his meal today. I'm sorry, Phillipa. I know you had higher hopes for him."

Phillipa shrugs, more occupied with her squash casserole than the elderly gentleman carrying Leslie's legs or Conrad hooking his arms under Leslie's shoulders to carry him not to one of the couches or into the full bathroom or the main suite but to the door behind Mother.

I strain to glimpse what's on the other side when Papa's wife rushes to open the door for the two men. I see stone walls, which makes no sense. Stone like that is only common as an exterior accent or on a mantel, and white limestone is more common in this area than the gray river stone in the other room. That's all I catch before the door swings shut.

I hear nothing from the room, nothing until the door opens again and the two men return without Leslie. For all I know, they've tossed him into a large freezer unit to die of exposure or suffocation, whichever comes first. And everyone just keeps eating, talking, laughing, drinking. Like the school cafeteria if we also had public hangings.

It's half past seven, and there's still an oven that hasn't been opened. I hope we're almost at desserts, but what do we do for four more fucking hours? Are we actually ahead of schedule? Will we get out before midnight?

Are we almost on the other side of this?

Zoe said the mutilations aren't normal, that they usually get through a feast without a hitch. As bad as it is, maybe this is as bad as it gets. Maybe we really can go home after drinking and eating our feelings, with leftovers like party favors—our doggy bags of bones.

It could have been so much worse.

Finish, spit, pass the red wine glass.

The servers pour a port wine this time. It smells and tastes sweeter, slightly metallic, or maybe that's just the scent of Tawna's blood caught in my nostrils.

Mother stands once more, her glass raised, and everyone falls silent, air thick and expectant, as though the fire in the hearth has burned too high and long and the flue is half shut.

"For those unfamiliar with our feasts, it might seem like we've just had the main event. But you already know we like to do things a little differently around here. Esoteric, some might call us. If enjoying fleshly things—pleasure, pain, variety—is esoteric, then fine, we're esoteric."

The crowd around the suburban sprawl of table laugh long and low, like moans, and Zoe kisses my shoulder, running her fingertips down my arm in a way that breaks me out in chill bumps.

In spite of my anger and fear, she turns my head. Layla clenches her teeth as Zoe kisses me again, deep, sweet as the port wine. I want her to stop so I can think; I don't want her to stop so I don't have to think, because all the paths my thinking mind traverses are haunted with the things I should have and should be doing, and none of them are happening here.

She cups my breast and lays her head on my shoulder, hair tickling my neck, to listen to Mother once more. Every time I breathe in, she shifts her palm until my nipple is hard underneath. With the pleasure surfaces discomfort, because I remember Conrad doing the same to Tawna. Perhaps Tawna remembers the same, because she silently pleads with me as she continues to force herself to eat the rest of the fortunately soft casseroles.

Conrad stares, too, meeting my eyes between glances at my other nipple trying to push through my knit top. He moves his hand under the table again, slow, luxurious strokes that emphasize length I can't see. My mouth goes dry as the white wine and wet as the red.

Mother continues when the laughter peters out. "We have a few more treats to go before we hit desserts, mine and whatever you want to grab from the dessert table. Our next course is another celebration of flesh. If you're inclined to finish something started a few courses back, you're welcome to the indulgence. Enjoy your bodies, family, friends—how they serve you, how they save you, how you beat and bleed and pulse and run with electricity, your bodies of salt, fat, protein, bone, marrow, the elements of you distilled and preserved and stimulated in meat. Everything you eat gives you strength, power, knowledge, memory, health…life. We respect the bodies, flora and fauna, that feed these bodies, and we serve our bodies to remember why we live our lives, such fragile things. We think we are forms of such matter, and yet we are paper held to flame under the right—or wrong—circumstances. For those who have sacrificed for our meal, we give our thanks."

I know. I know what's coming and refuse to know it. To let it form letters, much less words. To comprehend, hold, weigh it in my head. I know what they're going to bring out next, but neither knowing nor refusing to know prepares me for what's inside the third oven.

Three bald, roasted heads, with small plums in their cooked screams.

Father fusses with the dated sound system, a multi-disk CD player. The whole time, it's been playing some kind of soft smooth jazz so soft and so smooth I barely noticed it was on until he removes the CDs and replaces them with new ones. The jarring Motown cheeriness of the Supremes emanates from the speakers. He twists the volume up and snaps all the way back to his seat as Mother rests the head pan where she carved the turkey.

Family members clap with unbridled enthusiasm. Zoe, latched to my arm and humming along to the Supremes, occasionally deviates from the melody to express how delicious the heads look.

Next, Mother removes two pineapple-roasted, honey-glazed legs, from buttock to just above the knee. From the way it's cooked, it could be ham, but by length and shape, they're clearly human.

There's even a shallow pan full of cracklings at the bottom

of the oven.

With every exclamation of familial admiration, the guests finally realize the shit they've stepped in, wallowed in, and now have to swallow. Which means the people who brought them here told them about the orgy and extreme punishments, but they didn't warn that we would all become party to the worst of their predilections.

It shouldn't have really surprised us, though, that a family happy to serve people pieces of themselves would be just as happy to serve people to others. We thought we could escape unscathed. We *had* to believe that to convince ourselves to keep going, to endure the guilt and let others endure the pain and humiliation. Tears had been enough to put me in line.

If they're going to let us go, this is how they do it: By making us not just spectators but active participants in their crimes. Because that's what they are. Criminals, all of them, and this isn't the first time their table has been the scene of those crimes. They all but admit it to us in tradition, in fond memories, in the ease with which they engage in and encourage others to join in that tradition, share those memories.

Some guests struggle to stand in indignance. Now they cry. Now they protest.

But those of us who were prey to the family's behavior, from mild to extreme—me and, across, Tawna—remain where we are, our bodies stainless steel wires stretched almost to snapping.

Besides, Zoe's holding on too tightly, because she knew body parts would be leaving the oven. She knew this would be the part where the guests, glad it wasn't them, realize what's expected to keep it that way.

And this is also when the suburban cannibalistic family cult pulls out knives from their jackets, from sheaths latched to the back of their pants, from bras, and the threat of pretty faces marred, or worse, stops shocked guests in their tracks. Servers block the two apparent exits.

Meanwhile, Mother continues her work in the kitchen as though the commotion is to be expected during any normal gathering of family and friends.

At knifepoint, the roughly dozen guests who tried to escape return to their seats.

"Let me go, damn it!" One of the family's business buddies—Joel, I think—wrenches against the servers' hold. He's bigger than them, and afraid, but Mother is their incentive to keep him back. They will do anything for Mother, because they know and don't just guess what she'll do, and they're more afraid.

Mother is great; Mother is good. Let us thank her for our food. Amen.

"Don't worry, Sierra. It looks freaky, but it tastes really, really good, especially the ham." Zoe leans in to add in a whisper, "Better than the turkey, in my opinion. Ham should really be the star of Thanksgiving, not turkey."

"It's not ham. Don't call it ham. It's not ham." I'm shaking again. I brace against the waves of hot following cold.

"The cut's the same, and it's got similar notes, especially when you cook it the same," Zoe says, which extinguishes the thin possibility that she really believes the legs belong to slimmer hogs, the faces to juvenile pigs with their noses removed. She's not clueless, which means she's not blameless, not even slightly. "Just wait until you try the cracklings."

"Skin, Zoe. Cracklings are fried skin."

"Air-fried. Less trans fat than deep-fried."

"Trans fat isn't the problem. I didn't come to an American Thanksgiving to eat American skin. Do you really not realize that this is wrong, Zoe? Someone had to die for your dinner."

Zoe shakes her head with a laugh of disbelief. "Something always has to die for dinner. Everything that gives you nutrients has to die—plants, animals, fungi. No one lives without a little murder."

"Not people. We're not supposed to eat people."

"Stop being so anthropocentric, Sierra. We have no more or less right to live here than anything else. Humans shape the world, cover it in inedible mineral, and we think we're the puppet masters. But here, we eat of the body and drink of the blood and call it good because it tastes good. Why else do we do anything except because we can?"

As soon as they can foist Joel upon the couple who invited him, the servers take the heads and put each on their own separate platter, then bring them to the table, one for each side and one in the middle. Closer to those they serve, they slice through the forehead and cheeks.

The lashes and eyebrows were removed along with the rest of the hair before cooking, and the eyelids were slow roasted almost shut. As the server reveals more of the skull like some morbid striptease, I can't help but compare the sight to the fresher meat of Tawna's face.

Another server provides small bowls of more giblet gravy

at everyone's place. Tender piece by piece, the servers carving heads fill the plate of each person in his section. Those comfortable with his performance offer their plate, then offer the plate of guests who continue to resist, yelling over their friends and Diana Ross.

"I'm not eating people!"

"What do I look like, a psycho psychiatrist?"

"You're crazy! They were right. You're all crazy!"

"Let me go! Let me fucking go, you motherfucker."

"Take your Soylent Green and stick it up your ass with a corkscrew!"

"This has gone too far!"

You think?

Speaking calmly and rationally about it with someone I like and who likes me got me nowhere. I don't expect that flinging obscenities like monkey poo is going to change minds any time soon, especially since no one in the room—not me, not the grown-ups—has a stone to throw in this glass house.

"Remember what we talked about in the beginning, sweetie." Zoe kisses my cheek, the way she did when I stressed over midterms. "Follow the rules, and you'll be fine. If you get through these courses, you reach the end of the maze, which is pie."

"Where is the pie, Zoe? All three ovens have been full with meat and sides."

"They're in the proofing oven or chilling in the fridge. Mother made them two days ago. Sierra, what's going on? Are you sure you're feeling okay?" Zoe presses the back of her hand against my forehead. "You still don't have a fever. Look, there's no grand conspiracy here. We're just a family with our own way of doing things, and it seems to serve us well. I mean, there are theories about why it serves us well. The more superstitious among us think we take in other people's strength, fate, and fortune and can spend it for ourselves. I think that's bullshit. I think the reason why we work is that we don't have the same obstacles everyone else has to accomplish things; to be perfectly blunt, we're cutthroat."

She slices through the forehead on her plate, dips it in the gravy, and eats it with slightly less irony than if she had some of the neck. "Not always so literally. We succeed because we don't care what others think, and we never forget we're family, legal or found. We have a little bit of everything so that we want for nothing—our own family stew. If you get through this, Sierra, you're not thousands of miles away from family. We're right here. And you get to have those adventures and new experiences that you wanted. Come on, you'd never be able to get your hands on this most places in the world—not so well cooked. Try it."

She cuts from one of the cheek slices on my plate, dips it lightly in the gravy—to flavor rather than drown, which would have been my first line of defense against what I have to do— then brings it to me, her hand underneath to catch the drips.

She still looks like my Zoe. She still sounds like my Zoe. She still feels like my Zoe. But I've only known her for four months, and though it may feel like longer, there's so much I don't know.

I don't know how Mother punished her as a child, how she encouraged her, *what* she punished and encouraged. I don't know what the kids are doing at the kids' table, whether they have to eat the same things, if they know what it is. I don't know at what age she joined the grown-ups' table, with Mother and Father's blessing, and what she tells herself about what happened during those holidays. I don't know what she does when she's not in the dorm room. I know what she *says* she does, and I know who she is with me, but now I'm seeing who she is when she has a hundred other mirrors reflecting different angles of her that I've never seen when sitting right in front of her.

I don't know what god she worships, because there's no church built to them. I don't know what her communications degree is for. I don't know who finds the people they kill or who does the deed. I don't know who she's taken into her body with such relish or the tears she's sown into the soil under cemetery stone.

She's a sensitive-eyed mystery to me, and on one hand, parts of me find that danger more interesting than it has any right to be, because those parts don't care about how that danger applies to me. On the other hand, how I feel doesn't matter. Whether I like her or it's just a crush, she's a portion of the key that will help me make it out alive. What I choose to do is what fits into the lock.

I open my mouth and don't close my eyes as she guides the meat onto my tongue. I bite steel to take the gravied cheek into my mouth. I remember Tawna chewing on her own and the pain of it, but this is painless, and it tastes as good as promised, which is even worse. My mouth waters in its eagerness to break the flesh down faster.

Zoe smiles, brilliant as a jack-o'-lantern. "Good, isn't it?"

I hear disgust around the table. Tawna's disappointment and Conrad's desire burn their respective holes into me, but the only one whose feelings I'm interested in is in the kitchen, still carving through the long ham. Although Mother doesn't smile, it reaches her eyes anyway, along with the smoothing lines that signal relief.

Because any crime in which I implicate them, I now implicate myself.

I mustn't offend my hosts.

Like a domino line, my acquiescence leads to the compliance of the rest. Complaints and protests still pour from their lips, chased by whimpers, but the slow-cooked flesh of strangers fall down their dark throats. Even Tawna, whose weary, overworked, understaffed muscles leave her in constant pain every time they move, takes the hairless scalp served. She douses it in gravy to ease the slide when she can't chew, but it's such tender flesh because it's been given the time necessary, with the right preparation. After all, Mother said she'd been working on the menu for a week.

As I eat from the head and from the cracklings—which are all the salt I could ask for—I stare into the jellied eyes of the person I consume. De-bristled and cooked, it's hard to tell: Were they man or woman? Were they a transient or a professional that the family used in some capacity, like home nurse, house cleaner, landscaper, rideshare or delivery driver? Or someone who just happened to walk by the house in the dark when Mother's keen eyes caught them, and she took them down with machete in hand? Or, like their recruits, do family members choose who they want to eat and make it look like an innocuous missing? No one would ever suspect Mother or Father of what they do. Put a lacy cap on Mother and a white beard on Father, and they could be Mr. and Mrs. Claus tomorrow, when they start celebrating Christmas.

Perhaps the person eaten at the other end, with gusto or garish cringe, was an accountant who filed taxes poorly. Perhaps the person chewed upon in the center forgot to lock a back gate. Perhaps the person in front of me flirted with the wrong father's daughter. Perhaps I've seen their faces on a report or a Missing Persons board.

Perhaps I even know them.

Zoe scoops out an eye with her spoon, then giggles as she bites into it to release the fluid that slow roasting hasn't dehydrated. "It doesn't taste very strong, but it's like meat jelly."

Matt takes the other one.

The woman on the other side of Duke coughs, then retches. Reeling away, Duke pushes me into Zoe, who pushes into Matt, who almost falls off the end of the bench next to Layla, the only person in the whole fucking room who I think fully comprehends the depravity committed over the years. At the foot of the table, she bears witness, helplessness rooted in her from years of watching her family win.

She should be the most significant evidence to keep me in my place—albeit displaced, crushed by Duke and crushing Zoe in turn. Both of them laugh at the position we've found ourselves in as the woman next to Duke expels head meat, casseroles, and some traditional dinner onto her plate. It spills over onto the placemat, bile-sour brown gravy soup with Thanksgiving chunks, marbled with cranberries and red wine.

Mother drops her carving knife and fork and retrieves an unslotted silver serving spoon from a drawer. She leans over the table to hand it to the woman.

"You can't be serious," the woman sobs, still gagging. As though this, finally this, crosses the line. As though after everything we've seen and gone through, she still doesn't realize there isn't a line at all.

"You eat what I serve you," Mother says.

The woman stabs a finger in my direction. "You didn't make *her* eat what she threw up."

Both Duke and Zoe wrap their arms around me, forming a shield with their bodies. I'd be touched if I could feel any emotion at all.

"It's because your daughter brought her, isn't it?" the woman says. "You gave her a pass because your daughter's fucking her."

Mother hits her across the face with the spoon, holding nothing back. She's strong beneath her comforting softness. Swelling immediately rises, closing lids around the expanding blood-struck eye like curtains.

"Sierra flushed hers down the toilet, she didn't make a mess, and the reason why she threw up was because she's not accustomed to alcohol. The younger adults sometimes have this issue. That and illness are acceptable reasons to throw up. But you...you vomited because what I made disgusts you. Sierra here isn't throwing up now because she finds the origin of the meat distasteful. Even Tawna, who can barely chew, is eating the meat I serve her. And there isn't an epidemic of gastroenteritis at my table. This tells me that the problem, Gloria, is you. Now, you can use the spoon or we can get a turkey baster and that bite spreader. But I simply can't abide a weak stomach at my table. How do you think these people would feel, to have their parts so vilely wasted? *Eat.*"

Mother thrusts the spoon at the woman again.

Duke nudges me, grabs his plate, and indicates that I should do the same. "This part is hilarious," he whispers, "but there tends to be a splash zone."

I pick up my plate and wine glass, and Duke and I move between Matt and Layla like spectators with popcorn. There's no good way to use a knife and fork while standing. Duke just finger-foods it, dipping slices into his gravy and grabbing new pieces as the server finishes stripping the skull. I slowly round Layla and lay my plate on the table next to her. I cut the meat and try not to rubberneck, but I can't help it.

Gloria sobs and gags through gathering the vomit together to put the partially digested acidic soup back in her mouth. She pushes it as far back as possible, so she won't have to taste it, but the chunks stimulate her gag reflex every time. I can smell the acid sting from here, so it has to be worse there.

The body rejects things for a reason. There might not be anything poisonous in the meat, but her body is convinced there is. It comes back up more than once, splattering on the plate and dribbling over her chin.

As she resumes carving, Mother keeps a watchful eye.

When the swelling in the eye and not just the socket reaches a red-weeping pitch and Gloria can't eat for screams, Pasquale comes up behind with a swizzle stick and stabs her between the eyelids. The pressure releases in another spray that hits Conrad right in his face with blood and humor. He roars with laughter, and his friend next to him slaps him on the back like he caught a homerun at a baseball game.

Now Gloria is screaming and screaming, loud enough to wake the dead.

Layla doesn't even flinch as she focuses on the food on her plate, her motions perfunctory and without variation. Stab, dip, chew, chew, chew, chew, swallow, stab, dip, chew, chew, chew, chew, swallow, sip, sip, sip, lather, rinse, and repeat.

A server who finishes carving his head goes to the back room where they took Leslie. He returns with a mouth retractor and bite opener, which he forces into her while her deflated eyeball weeps through shiny swollen lids that will become a black eye, if she lives that long. Mother pauses her carving to hand the turkey baster, liquid clinging in beads to the insides, to Father, who passes it off to one of the servers.

They force her head back while she screams and hiccups and chokes on tears and mucus flowing to the back of her mouth.

In the absence of the football game, the family bets against her, passing bills between them when she gurgles and vomits again from the turkey baster touching her throat. The server has to push her forward so she doesn't drown. When they manage to get all the liquid down and her plate is only chunks, the servers gather it up in the serving spoon and tilt it into her mouth, telling her to swallow, swallow, swallow. The captive audience joins in the chant, even some of the guests, swept up in the manic joy and desperately glad that they're not the ones causing it.

There's nothing I can do for Gloria. What happens to her is out of my hands. I can't get complacent about it, because Mother really could have made me drink toilet water in the absence of expelled food. She could have made me re-eat everything from the first course to the main meal, because she has plenty of leftovers. I'd borrow from some of the more religious Christians on campus and claim *but for the grace of God*, but I don't think God is here, and if He is, like Layla, He averts his eyes.

I focus on cleaning my plate without letting the awful gagging and vomiting trigger my own reflex, which seems to be a problem for others at the table, who cover their mouths and force themselves to swallow it back again. A moment's sour is bad enough, but the prospect of such humiliation makes them resolute to keep their gorge heavy and low.

I take the plum from between the skull's teeth. Better than an eye.

Mother finishes with the legs. Bones go into the bone container. She arranges the meat, which doesn't look like ham on the inside, on a long platter with halved pineapple slices. From the fridge, she retrieves meat already cut into strips and fires up the stove again, where she arranges the cast-iron pan, maple syrup, apple cider vinegar, and cracked pepper in which to cook the bacon.

Zoe still has my purse and may have stashed it somewhere beneath the bench, but it'll be suspicious if I try to retrieve it. Zoe knows I'm not on my period. There's no reason for me to need my purse for anything but lip balm at this point in the night. I have to let it go if I'm going to do this.

Mother stands at the stove, supervising the caramelization of pale bacon. It smells incredible.

My whole gut cramps enough to make me double over, and I worry that I actually do need to use the bathroom again, but the cramps soon subside without forcing an issue. I wish I could have more sparkling juice, but instead, I finish my wine and leave my plate on the corner. I still hold my fork and knife, but only up to the island where Mother carved the legs. Shaking, I trade my cutlery for the carving knife and two-pronged carving fork—carefully, without a shuffle or a clang.

My own breath seems unbearably loud, but if I hold it for too long, I'll faint, and that would be worse than getting caught, because then I'd be caught and unconscious.

Mother doesn't hear me over the sizzle, and everyone else is too occupied with the Gloria game for them to care about me going off toward the bathroom again, especially since I finished my plate of person face, family dues paid. If any guests do notice, I hope they cheer me on in their heads the way I would if roles were reversed.

I creep toward the opening to the front of the house, holding the carving tools near my body so their gleam won't catch attention, and so there's a chance I can hide them if no one's looking too closely.

I'm in the hallway, halfway to the foot of the stairs, when Mother calls through the buzzing quiet. "Still feeling queasy?"

I don't turn my body, just my head, and hope she doesn't see handles sticking out beneath my fists. "Not anymore. But between the juice and the wine, I do need to use the bathroom again.”

“You don’t want to miss dessert.”

I feel Zoe in her stare, as though her daughter can see through her eyes. It makes it difficult to lie. I convince the slight pressure in my bladder to intensify so she doesn’t glimpse a hint of guilt.

“I’ll be back in a sec.”

I go to the powder room and close the door behind me, then lock it. They can force it open if they really want to, but for now, I’m safe—locked in a nine-square-foot room with a toilet and sink and little else. I lay the carving utensils across the top of the sink, push down my leggings, and pee, now that I’ve convinced my bladder I need to. I wait a few minutes to determine if the cramping in my gut leads to anything I need to worry about, but my intestines stay quiet.

I try to hear the sound of footsteps, of breathing other than my own. I search for shadow at the crack under the powder room door.

As far as I can tell, Mother doesn’t suspect anything and no one’s checking on me, and I’m left in a cool, quiet, peaceful place to think, where it’s easier to believe that what’s going on in the den isn’t happening, or at least not as I remember it. That I misinterpreted it somehow.

It would be so easy to lie to myself and say I’m overreacting. The bacon is just bacon. The ham is just ham. I love honey-roasted ham. The heads were those of roast-distorted pigs. Odd cuisine, to be sure, but every family has quirky traditions that don’t make sense on the outside.

American or not, every family is a little bit strange. Because everything that's happened is impossible, surely my memories are inaccurate, possibly prejudiced.

But the mirror doesn't let me pretend. Blood that's not mine flecks my face. Vomit that's not mine flecks my sleeve. Hollow eyes, hollow stare of a century of horrors, like someone collected tragedies and stuffed them into the body of an eighteen-year-old girl, but it doesn't fit in there right among all the things supposed to be there instead.

The dorm this morning feels like twenty years ago. How am I still the same person, except flat, bland, lifeless but for a heady flush on my cheeks—perhaps from wine? This is not the face of someone who misinterpreted. Things are not fine.

I may never eat again.

So, really, what have I got to lose?

I pick up the carving utensils again, one in each hand, and ease open the door. No one's waiting for me when I peek out. I'm free all the way to the front door, as long as nobody's on the stairs or in the kitchen opening.

I sneak out, still glancing in every direction. No one in the parlor hiding in the shadow of the chairs, waiting like an assassin. No one on the stairs, not even kids sneaking down to see how the other half lives. I stay as close to the right as I can, out of view of the kitchen, but to reach the front door, I have to risk exposure and put both utensils in one hand so the other is free for the door handle.

My heart threatens to vibrate right out of my chest and scurry into the walls like a cockroach, but I've already come this far.

I dart to the door and undo the deadbolt, then pull the handle.

"I had high hopes for you, Sierra." Mother leans against the wooden paneling that lines the hall to the kitchen, her arms crossed like she's caught me coming in after curfew, and for a moment, I feel like I'm the one who's done something wrong. I want to stop and explain, talk my way out of punishment, as though all that's going to happen is two weeks grounded and no screentime after homework.

I yank open the front door and run out without bothering to close the door behind me. It'll slow me down more than them.

I don't yell for help. I don't expect anyone to hear me. Even if they do, they'll probably think it's a prank or a coyote. Whole houses might be empty because the neighbors are traveling for Thanksgiving. On top of that, I can't know how many neighbors have been to one of these Samuels holiday feasts, or how many are here now. I can't trust anyone. But if I can just get out and into a public place where they're less likely to have influence, I'll have a better chance of making it out of this alive.

I'm not even off the front porch before a powerful hand grabs me by my hair. I scream, but not to be heard. His hold threatens to rip off my scalp.

Not one of the servers, but Conrad, still splattered with blood. He drags me back into the house like I'm made of foam. One of the servers shuts the door and locks the deadbolt. That's not really what keeps me in, but the clunk is final as a gavel.

I whirl around, moving with Conrad's hold on me instead of against it. That catches him off guard enough for me to thrust the carving knife into his right side.

This time, the blood blooming on the white shirt is his own, and his roar isn't from laughter.

Mother isn't the only one watching anymore. A crowd of shadows clusters in the kitchen, struggling to see—wide-eyed guests and glinting family, despair and damnation all in one after-dinner coffee. I can't see Zoe, but perhaps that's for the best—for me more than her.

Conrad clutches his side. The blade was made for sawing, not stabbing. Impeded by his clothing, it stabbed too shallowly. "You're a lot feistier than I expected after you crumbled under Mother's scolding. Eat your vegetables. Do your homework. Scream a little louder for me, darling, and try to stab me again. That one almost tickled."

He still has a hold on my hair, and the server comes up from behind to take me by the arms and neutralize the weapons. I duck away and push closer to Conrad, who doesn't mind when I wrap my arms around his waist to avoid the server. He falls back on the stairs, laughing and wincing in turns.

The kids heard the commotion. Some of them have run down *almost* to the landing, but their respect and fear of Mother means not even curiosity will catch them with one toe crossing the boundary between the kids' space upstairs and the adults below.

They still have a front-row seat, better than the grown-ups in the kitchen, as I stab the carving fork straight into Conrad's junk. I can't say whether it gets his cock, his balls, or just his abdomen. Either way, he's not laughing anymore, and I don't think he'll get too excited to look at me going forward.

It pleases me to the viscera to have him not shout or roar but howl at an octave he would never choose, the entirety of his mind and body narrowed to the crude castration. At the very least, I've ruined his day, and if that's all I accomplish tonight, after everything I've willingly done, that's a gift I don't deserve. I leave the fork in him and slash instead at everything I can reach—his chest, his arms when he builds up the wherewithal to defend more than his balls, his pretty face.

I hope he fucking scars. I hope he thinks he's hideous. And I keep slashing as the server finally gets a solid hold, hooking his arms under mine and locking my shoulders so I can't swing in front of me, only to the sides.

He tightens his hold and shakes me hard, like a ketchup bottle, until he jostles the carving knife from my hand. It clatters on the hardwoods but lands with a sigh on the foyer rug.

The server has such a good grip on me that I let him carry my weight as I kick at Conrad trying to come after me, kick at the banister to push me and the server back toward the front door, kick at Mother as she approaches me like a trainer with a skittish horse.

"Stay away from me! Everyone stay away!"

I intimidate no one without a weapon—not the server, not Mother, although Conrad falls back against the stairs, clutching his crotch once again and leaving stains on the stair runner. Not as easy as a rug to wash, but I'll bet Mother has fool-proof methods for getting even the most stubborn red stains out of carpet.

"I just want to go home. Please, Mother, I just want to go home. I want to go home to my mom. I want my mom. Please let me go home. *Please.*"

I'm still kicking, still struggling, but despair weighs my limbs like honey. Not even adrenaline can fool me into thinking there's a way out of this.

I took my shot and missed.

From behind her back, Mother pulls out a syringe with a needle as thick and long as a stirring straw. "This isn't supposed to mix with alcohol, but I suppose needs must. Hold her still, Jacob. She should never have gotten this far. Try not to be so distracted next time."

She sticks the needle into my neck with unnerving ease.

The world does more than tilt like it did before I vomited. Oh, it tilts. It also whirls. It's a Tilt-A-Whirl. I don't know which way is up as I struggle to put my feet back beneath me.

"I'd almost be proud if I weren't so disappointed."

Mother becomes my swirling center as she frames my face on my way to the ground. I never understood why eyes roll back in a faint, but now I do. I follow the world as it falls back into my eye sockets.

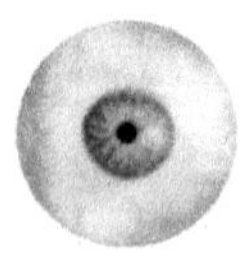

Where I awaken, there are no windows, only artificial light. I can't tell if I've been out for an hour or a week. I'm wearing the same clothes I came to the Samuels' house in. My shoes are designed for sitting and that's mostly what I did all day, but my feet are starting to hurt and I long for grass between my toes.

Everything hurts, like I've run ten miles, even though I didn't even run two steps. Everywhere there's muscle, skin, joint, I ache.

I try to stretch, but the straps on my arms and legs don't allow much range of movement, although they're well-padded and smooth leather, so insidiously binding that I didn't immediately know I was bound—the kind that cares how comfortable they are for the captive, rather than rough jute or zip ties.

The idea of considerate captors doesn't comfort me.

Between aches, pains, and the blinding cone of disorienting clarity pouring over me, I'm hardboiled and overexposed. I find freckles I didn't know I had, the finest organic grid of my skin delineated. I strain to see more beyond the light, but it doesn't dare expose the rest of the room with more than suggestion and glowing electronic eyes.

When the rest of the lights switch on, they flood the room like water. I squint against the added brightness, even though the lights on the other side of the cone aren't actually that bright. But they illuminate gray river stone.

I'm in the back room.

Based on size and the fact the room is a little lower than the den, the floor unpolished concrete, I think the room used to be a garage in a former life. However, there's no sign of a garage door. The river stone looks solid.

In addition to river stone, several glass door refrigerators, a glass door walk-in freezer, and two large icebox units line the wall in front of me. Against the wall to my right are six industrial ovens and two rotisserie ovens. I assume they have a whole barbecue and smoker kitchen in their backyard. They seem like the kind of family who would barbeque on July 4th, before gathering around a gas firepit to make s'mores. Maybe they even have a pizza oven—a whole outdoor cooking experience to match the one inside.

Not that I can figure out yet how they would get to the backyard, with no doors to it in the den.

It doesn't really matter, because there's an autopsy table under caged pendant lights like mine. Sterile and shiny, the frosted metal makes an amorphous ghost of me. Against the back wall is a pegboard of torture objects—or kitchen tools. The witches were right—the Venn diagram of those things is a circle.

Several people enter through the den door. Someone shuts the door and locks it twice, first with a deadbolt, then a key. I try to hear the feast, or the commentator chatter of the game. There's nothing.

Maybe all their mouths are full.

Multiple footsteps descend a small set of stairs.

"The party is over. Except for immediate family, most everyone's gone home." Mother is in front of me, and I whip back around so she can't do anything before I can see—although maybe that would be a mercy. "Usually, I'd offer you a mimosa and brunch after staying over, but you haven't finished your Thanksgiving meal yet.”

I throttle the impulse to beg again. It’s not going to change anything. Mother makes her own reality. She’s the god her daughter prays to.

“And I do apologize for that.” As polite as I can be while considerately bound. “I was looking forward to pie.”

“As well you should. I make wonderful pie.”

Mother drags a loose chair across to me and perches on its edge. My chair is bolted to the floor. She sits partially in my cone of light and partially out. Her shoes are starkly etched. She wears transition lenses like her daughter’s. They’re darkened to protect her from the glare.

“Sierra, I’m not embarrassed to admit that I’m confused.” Mother rests her hands on her legs, palm over her knuckles like a therapist. “You had two courses to go before the feast finished. The ham and bacon are the saltiest. You would have enjoyed them. And dessert is communal, player’s choice along with the dessert buffet. You could have gone around the table, met new people with your pie. We make Irish coffee, hot buttered rum, hot chocolate, and popcorn. We watch the game. We package the leftovers. It’s great fun and much less structured than the rest of the feast. Two more courses. Instead, you tried to leave the feast early, without even informing your hosts or the person who brought you here. Why would you do that?”

“Why would you do that to *me*?” Zoe creeps out from the corner near the locked door, her shoulders hunched like she’s afraid of being kicked. I’ve never seen her look so vulnerable. Hell, hurt.

She changed into pajamas at some point, a dab of red in my view. Christmas pajamas. It's the day after Thanksgiving. They're putting up the tree tonight.

We didn't bring clothes with us, and she said nothing about staying the night, so maybe she borrowed from one of her sisters. Zoe wearing pajamas doesn't narrow down the time, but Mother said something about brunch, so maybe it's late morning the day after.

Even if my parents don't get a call on Sunday, they won't freak out. They'll just assume I finally have a life. They'll congratulate me to each other thousands of miles away from whatever shallow grave I'm buried in. If Zoe doesn't report me missing, it might take longer than a week for the professors to notice that someone who never seemed flaky before isn't showing up for classes or turning in essays. How long can she hold off reporting it before the delay seems suspicious?

Mother stands and holds up her hand to stop Zoe from getting closer. "I told you to stay over there."

Zoe crosses her arms like a breastplate. "I just want to know the same thing you do."

"I couldn't handle the marathon." I keep my tone light and polite, as even as I can when my voice threatens to waver. "I wanted to go home and miss my family in the dark and quiet of our dorm room."

"Why didn't you just say that?" Zoe asks.

"Because we stay until the feast is over. That's the rule."

"We could have come up with something. There are quieter rooms in the house. We could have finished in the parlor. We could have finished in my bedroom. You couldn't call family until after the feast, but you were so close to reaching the end. Honestly, you couldn't make it two more damn courses?"

"I was leaving the feast, Zoe, not you."

"Why?" Zoe stays so far away from me, her shoulders almost on the river stone. She's beautiful, scrubbed and unadorned. I've always thought so. Her hair is wild in the morning, and she takes selfies like that sometimes, genuinely able to say she woke up that way, with the kind of bedhead usually only money can buy. "Why would you do that when you knew what would happen if you did? Why would you do that to me?"

"I had to try. I don't expect you to understand. But it wasn't about you."

"Of course it was about us," Mother says. "I know we're not what you're used to, but don't insult us further by saying it's not us you were trying to escape."

"It wasn't Zoe I was trying to escape," I correct her.

But that's not entirely true, either, is it? Because Zoe's firmly knotted on their tree, and if she's part of the family, she's part of the feast. I can't have Zoe without the feast.

"Fair enough," Mother says. "But what made you think you could escape?"

"I didn't think I could. I just knew I had to try."

"That's not what I meant. What did you think you were escaping?"

"I didn't want to eat anyone else. I didn't want to watch your family torture people for fun. I wanted to let someone know what was happening here. I wanted you to stop. I don't think that was asking for much, but I knew you weren't going to let me just walk out. I had already asked Zoe, and she basically said no. You're not going to let any of us go, not your guests, and especially not the ones you punish. You can't. We're evidence. We're proof."

Mother sits again. Zoe stays out of reach, almost out of sight if I look at Mother instead.

"You're sorely mistaken, Sierra. Of course we're going to let you go. We don't even have to make you eat your tongue to do it. I apologize for the discomfort you must be feeling, but the sedative was the only way to make sure you didn't disturb the feast for the rest of us. Oh, I could have made an example of you right there, like the others. But I'll admit, I'm both kinder and tougher on my daughters, and I can tell how much she likes you. I wouldn't want to cause her the same public distress as you so callously did. Do you see any of the other vulgarians in here?"

The room is empty, except for a pig—definitely a pig, not just something they're calling a pig—hanging on a meat hook in the freezer. Their own private butchery. They brought Leslie back here, but he isn't here now—either whole or in pieces— as far as I can tell.

Just Mother, Zoe, me, and the pig.

"What did you do with them?"

Mother laughs. "What do you think we did with them? We let them go."

"Bullshit." Not a word I normally use around parents who aren't my own.

Mother sighs, as though I'm a child pushing boundaries, not an almost-adult who made a deliberate decision.

"Oh, Leslie was mostly unconscious, Gloria still felt ill, and Tawna was, as you know, a mess, so they couldn't just walk out the door. We give them drugs to make them forget, and after a brief clean, we leave them where they'll be found and tended to. They won't remember the feast. They may not even remember who they are for a while. But we don't hunt from our own table, Sierra. We would never invite people to our home and, for their rudeness, repay them double with the same. They will likely live—no reason why they shouldn't. Now, if you'd killed my cousin, perhaps we'd be having a different conversation."

She nodded to the autopsy table.

"He does tend to be overzealous with the wrong guests; I suppose every family has someone like him. I understand if you took his behavior personally and responded in kind. But that doesn't mean your actions don't have consequences. You saw enough to know this was coming if you were caught."

"Zoe…" I strain against the bindings. "You know I just wanted to go home."

She doesn't move, barely looks at me. "And you knew you would get to go home. You still get to go home. Just not the same way you left it."

"Zoe…"

"I'm so mad at you right now, Sierra." Her jaw is tense, her throat tight. She's on the brink of tears. "We could have had such a good long weekend. We could have done all kinds of things. You could have just kept the secret in your stomach, in your bloodstream, in your bones, like the rest of them – silence, for the promise of greater reward and an indefinite seat at our venerated table. But you weren't here for the reward like them. You were here for me, and I brought you here for you. Then you threw that in the trash like we were your cheap sugar cookies."

"I don't throw cheap sugar cookies in the trash."

Zoe insulting my weak contribution to the dinner actually upsets me. It was one thing when she thought it was funny, another when she thinks it's gauche.

"And don't pretend this was for me," I snap. "You did this *to* me. You weren't sure how willing I'd be, with or without booze. You thought it was the only way to force-forge some kind of relationship—trauma-bonding or something. You wanted me in on the secret so I'd be ruined for anyone else but you. If this had been about me, you would have told me exactly what you were bringing me into. Instead, you let Mother humiliate me, then made me watch a man's hand get cut off and fed to him before you explained anything—and certainly not everything. You knew that if you explained to me what your family explains to everyone else, I would have had Thanksgiving in the cafeteria and been in bed watching *Supernatural* by ten, which sounds like heaven right now— cheap, easy, and I wouldn't know what a person's *face* tastes like."

"And other things. We sprinkle a few of those in here and there, for flavor." Mother leans back in the chair, deceptively relaxed. "I'm sorry, however, if the soup was insufficiently seasoned. I really might have spared too much salt, but I was too ashamed to say so in front of guests when I pride myself on the perfect menu." She flits her gaze to her daughter. "Zoe, you don't have to stay for this part. Take a hot bath, drink some chamomile. You'll want to be calmer when the time comes."

Zoe still doesn't move for a while, but Mother goes silent, and I have nothing more to say. My chest hurts too much for words, like someone's pulling on all my veins to find their center. She twitches, as though having second thoughts. Then she climbs the stairs and locks the door behind her.

"You're smarter than your timidity makes you seem," Mother says quietly. "I advised Zoe to bring you to one of our weekend dinners first—more casual, lower stakes. You might never have known what you were eating, and you could have used whatever condiments or seasonings you wanted. I told her to be perfectly clear about expectations and motives—like in any good relationship. But at her age, all a mother can do is advise. She's got to make her own decisions, her own mistakes. She thought if she told you the truth, even an abbreviated version, you wouldn't come. Don't judge her too harshly. She likes you quite a lot."

"That makes it worse."

Mother nods as she considers her nails—meticulously cared for but unmanicured. A good cook uses their hands too much for lacquer. "She's certainly not the first daughter who thought I might go easier on someone they like—or love—if that person came in without enough knowledge to be held fully accountable."

Empty pale eyes, hands and arms like mine, medicated to the gills. "Layla."

Mother leaves her chair to go to one of the ovens, set low to warm a plate—slices of leg with pineapple garnish and candied bacon, crispier than it might have been last night. She carries its tantalizing smell behind me.

It's funny how you can eat and eat and eat during a holiday, and you think you won't eat for a week, but there you are, picking at leftovers for lunch.

Something slides like a body across the concrete, but when Mother rounds me, it's just a table with legs designed to notch beneath my chair—a dinner tray. There's a paper napkin, a glass of water without ice, and a fork. No knife.

"I did most of the damage with a fork," I say.

Mother pats me on the shoulder. "Eat up, Sierra. You have a feast to finish."

"That's not all."

"No, it's not. But there's no reason why you should miss a wonderful meal."

"Even if I don't remember it?"

"On some level—perhaps cellular—you will. And maybe you and my daughter can have a better beginning that way. With some accommodations you never planned for, of course, but that shouldn't stop something real, should Zoe still wish to pursue you."

"What's going to be left of me to love?" The bacon is sticky between my fingers, the pepper coarse.

"You'll need your strength. Eat up."

Mother leaves me alone with a stranger's leg and belly delicious on my plate. When she returns, you can barely tell there was anything on the plate to begin with. She searches for any sign that I tried to get out of eating it or threw a tantrum by strewing the meat around. But for all I know, there's a camera in the room that allows her to watch me, and I'm doing no more damage than I've already done.

"I brought you your share of the brains." Mother sets a bowl of scrambled eggs with what looks like chicken sausage on the tray. "We broke open the skulls after you lost consciousness."

"What do you believe? Do you think you absorb the strength or knowledge or spirit of the people you eat?" The scramble could use some gravy, but I know better than to ask for more than the salt and pepper provided in the dish.

"Well, that's true of everything, isn't it? We eat to nourish our bodies, so our hearts can beat and blood can flow, so our brains and nerves can fire bioelectricity. Strength, knowledge, spirit… That isn't metaphysical. It's just physical." Mother joins me at the table with her chair again. "Some people find food a religious experience, and why not? Food isn't just nutritional; it's social, ritual, psychological, emotional. It's serotonin and dopamine. It makes you feel good. Gives you that warm feeling inside, even when you're eating ice cream. I believe food brings us closer to the divine, because we're meant to enjoy things in this world. Bread broken at any table is communion. A stove or oven is an altar. All that dies for your plate is a sacrifice."

"I don't think we're meant to enjoy people."

Her smile is gentle. "You seemed to enjoy the taste of my daughter just fine."

This is *not* a discussion I ever expected to be having with someone's mother, whether that someone was a boy or a girl. "I wasn't eating her."

"You were right there in front of us, Miss Sierra. Just because you didn't bite pieces off doesn't mean you weren't eating."

"Okay, fine." There isn't enough bleach to cleanse my mind, but it's already irreparably impure. "I don't think we're meant to kill people in order to enjoy them."

"Well, sometimes we don't," she said mildly. "But there are certain parts that require death, and it's more economical and practical to use all parts of one body than try to gather multiple parts from multiple bodies. Imagine if we only took a kernel from each ear of corn. The waste of it—like shark fin soup." Mother covers my hand before I can finish the scramble. "You won't convince me to let you go by telling me how wrong I am. I'm afraid that's a matter of perspective, and I find yours and the rest of the world's to be frustratingly narrow, puritanical, even dangerous."

"I'm the one who's dangerous?"

"I've seen you wield a fork."

"I've seen you wield one, too."

"You want pie?"

I'm startled into a stammer. "P-pie?"

"I have pumpkin, sweet potato, chocolate pecan, lemon meringue, and of course, classic apple. You can choose whatever combination and number of slices. Dessert course has always been more flexible."

"Sweet potato, chocolate pecan, and apple, please." I think pumpkin pies are too sweet, but I've never tried a sweet potato pie. I love pecans, don't like lemon meringue, and if I could grow an apple tree on the dorm balcony, I would. Also, the more I eat, the longer I delay what might be inevitable. "And can I have one of my sugar cookies? I don't care if no one else likes them. I do."

"Of course. And I'll bring a glass of milk. You can't have pie and cookies without milk."

She takes the bowl when I'm finished, leaving me alone again.

If she left the fork, maybe I would have something to work with, but I just have the table, which is of the same cheap material as anything in a college dorm room. I keep trying to slip my hands through my wrist bindings, but they're secure, designed to keep people from not hurting themselves while struggling hard enough to break their own bones.

The only way I'm getting out of here is if Mother slips up with utensils or undoes the bindings herself, and I don't think she'll give me the opportunity with either of those.

After Mother slides the dessert plate in front of me and sets the milk beside it, she undoes my left wrist restraint again and hands me a fork. "The rules of our table still apply. The flexibility of this situation doesn't extend that far."

Sweet potato tastes too much like pumpkin pie for me, just a different texture; I drink milk to help me swallow. The chocolate pecan is a good counterpoint to the sweet potato, with woodsy pecan and bitter chocolate cutting through the sweeter caramel.

And there's nothing in the world wrong with a good slice of apple pie.

After I finish with my cookie—which no one can make me feel guilty about liking—I drink down the rest of the milk, sipping rather than gulping, because I once again find myself with only one terrible chance.

I smash the milk glass as hard as I can on the edge of the dinner tray, because I'm afraid if I smash it on the plate, she'll make me eat the shards. Among the pieces, I pick the biggest, then shove the tray at Mother so I can lean down and saw at the binding at my left ankle. I don't care how the sharp edges cut into my palm or my leg, as long as it makes a dent in the padded leather and keeps all of Mother's attention. She's distracted by the bloody mess and the danger of the glass as I tuck my fork into the binding at my right wrist, the tines smooth against my forearm and the stem hidden in the heel of my palm.

I do manage to cut into some of the binding as well as a chunk of my leg that bleeds alarmingly red under such bright light, almost as though it isn't blood at all. The pain is negligible beyond the initial break through the skin, but I don't expect it to stay that way. Sometimes it takes the nerves a while to catch up, especially when a couple deep scrapes are the least of your problems.

Mother sweeps the rest of the shards to the side with her shoe, but she grabs my free wrist and fumbles with the larger shard, fights me for it until my blood makes us too slippery. Then she slams her sole into my knuckles, shoving the sharp points of the shard into my hand and leg but also neutralizing my hold. My fingers release, but I can't move. The shard remains in my leg, briefly defying gravity, but when she knocks it again, it falls to the ground. The more delicate parts break into smaller crumbs. She sweeps them away, too, panting.

"Goddammit!" Not a curse so much as an exclamation. Mother shakes her hand, smeared with her blood and mine from battling over broken glass.

I hiss from my now awakening nerves, but the leather padding is torn and tufted and there are scratches in the leather, some deep. Enough to break through? I don't think so, but each scratch is instability, a fault line to potentially exploit. It's worth the possibility, and the secreted weapon.

She runs to the sink behind the autopsy table and methodically washes her injuries. She cushions the cuts with gauze before wrapping a cloth bandage around the whole hand.

Then she brings the first aid kit to me.

A first aid kit and fire extinguisher in their slaughter room—safety first.

Mother binds my left hand back to the chair arm first, then tends to my leg above its binding best as she can. She uses skin glue for the more difficult cuts, then fortifies them with butterfly bandages and protects them all by wrapping the cloth bandage around my leg.

"Our surgeon left after the game," Mother says as she manages several basic sutures on my palm after irrigating the wounds for little glass pieces. "I'm unfortunately not in the practice of healing beyond knee scrapes, head bumps, and upset stomachs."

"Do you blame me?" I'm annoyed by how sincere the question is.

"No. You know what's coming. Because I'm kind, those I hunt never do." She pats my wrapped hand with hers. "But there's also no point in making this harder for you than it needs to be."

"You don't have to do this."

"If I set the rules, then don't follow through with the punishment, what does that teach my family? I'm already too lenient with my daughters. The last time I gave one too much rope, Layla almost hung herself with it. Everyone thinks they should be the exception, but you invited my punishment on purpose, Sierra. It would be cruel of me to deny you, or else the risk has no meaning. I'm going to get something to sweep up this glass. I'll be right back."

As soon as she's out of the room, I scrape the fork tines against the inside of the right wrist binding in a frantic sawing motion. I also tug against the left ankle binding, but the cuts that Mother couldn't reach underneath not only make my foot slippery—not enough to slip out—but they make every push against the leather like sparklers going off under my skin, tearing against attempts to clot.

I go still when I hear the key in the lock.

Mother sweeps the glass into a dustpan, tilts the pan into a trash bin, then meticulously wipes the floor of blood and milk except right under my shoe, because that's an endless, thankless task at this point. She leans close to the floor to check for any lingering grains of glass. Satisfied, she climbs back up with a groan.

"All right, my dear. You've eaten all the courses. If you're on tenterhooks about the game, I can bring in a laptop for you to watch the recording while we proceed with your punishment."

I shake my head. Maybe I could do with the distraction, but I think it would just end up souring me to the Cowboys.

My insides tell me that I need to use the bathroom, and I know what I've eaten, what my body has processed to the point it's ready to release what it can't use. Mother hears the gurgles, but she doesn't offer to unbind me.

I sense what's coming like the impending doom of a shelf cloud looming black and blue. Somehow, it's the humiliation that I dread more than pain, maybe because I can't imagine pain I've never had before.

Mother tilts her head for a moment. Then she moves behind me where I can't see her. I hear the slide of the trash bin beneath the chair. Then there's a sound like the swing of a trapdoor, and the chair shakes a little under me.

"I can't offer more than this. But I'm a mother, dear. I've done worse than wipe someone else's ass. If you need to go, now's the time."

"You can't be serious." Now *I'm* on the edge of tears.

"You've already proven yourself untrustworthy in a bathroom, and you might notice there isn't one back here." She pats my arm. Then she tucks up my shirt to grab the waistband of my leggings and my underwear. "It's better than the alternative, smart girl."

I whimper, clenching my eyes shut, but I shift my hips to make it easier for her to pull them halfway down my thighs, leaving my ass bare over empty space as though for a strapping. The weight of water, juice, wine, and milk pushes against the base of my bladder, but I can't convince myself to let go, and even more humiliatingly, I'm not sure I can convince my intestines *not* to let go, with the distress from the wine, possibly from the meat, and my conscience churning in my abdomen.

"I can't do this with you here." Tears, hot and stinging, escape down my face. "Please."

She's silent behind me.

"I can't. I physically can't." I can't even pee in an ocean where no one's watching, no one knows, and no one cares, least of all the fish doing the same and worse. My bladder will burst before I pee where someone can see; it's hard enough in communal bathrooms where they can hear.

Silence again. There's no reason for her to do anything to make me more comfortable. She certainly didn't for any of the other people they punished—at least not in ways those people would call comfortable.

"I'll be back in ten minutes."

I force myself to saw the tines into the cuffs while I ugly-cry. I'm not sure why this is the last straw for me, but maybe I don't get to decide that for myself.

I pee into a trash can full of milky glass. Then I shit in a way that would be unpleasant for me alone in my dorm bathroom, with music drowning out the sounds and my own misery, and an endless supply of anti-odor spray. I can't stop wailing off the hard walls, pulling against the bindings even though it hurts my leg and my hand aches and I'm sitting and shitting in the same chair I'm going to be tortured and might die in.

To Mother, this is mercy, and my bladder agrees. My brain knows that mercy doesn't have to be mutually exclusive with cruelty, just as salt intensifies sweet.

I sag forward in the bindings, still sawing, still wailing, when I hear the lock again. I can't stop crying myself into a mess of snot, but I stop sawing.

Mother enters with a bowl of warm soapy water and washcloths. I twitch when she starts cleaning me off, but I can't twitch far. I have no choice but to let her take care of me to get rid of that awful gritty itchiness and filth and stench. She dries me off, then pulls up my underwear and leggings again and latches the seat back up before taking the trash bin and its stink away. At the painter's sink, she washes her hands as well as she can with the bandages, then liberally sprinkles baking soda into the trash can.

"Zoe, you can come in now." Mother stays at the pegboard wall, considering her options as Zoe enters and relocks the door.

They're careful with the door, even though I'm bound. It speaks of ritual, as much a part of the recipe of this room as the altar walls and gleamingly clean stainless steel appliances fit for a restaurant.

"Please wipe her face while I prepare."

Zoe approaches with less defensiveness, as though her anger has deflated in the time it took for my insides to knot themselves like loose yarn. She uses a paper towel, not rough but thorough. There's almost tenderness when she tells me to blow my nose. Then she takes the rubber band out of her hair and combs mine back to tie it away from my face, allowing the air conditioning to cool my damp neck.

"You're going to want these." She sticks her hand in her

pocket, then opens the palm for a pair of oblong pills. "It's not an IV drip, but it'll help."

When she brings her hand to my mouth as though to keep me quiet, I accept the powdery pills onto my tongue. She lets me drink enough from a mini bottled water only to swallow.

"I'm going to be here the whole time." She covers my bandaged hand. "That's as much as I can do."

"Don't lie to yourself. And if you have any respect for me, don't lie to me, either."

"No, I really can't do anything else." Zoe sits in Mother's chair with a sigh. "There's no future where I can get you out of this. Layla tried. She brought her boyfriend home for Thanksgiving, and she tried to get around the rules, begged for Mother and Father to just drug him and let him go. Father had to hold her back while Mother redesigned his face, because he thought he could get out of retribution with a smile. She's never completely forgiven them, through the institutionalization or the therapy since, the lock on her bedroom door, other restrictions. She's a princess in a tower, and I still want to be able to forgive. This doesn't have to be an end, as long as we can make it through to the other side."

She isn't helping me control my tears, although after crying so much, I feel husked as an apple head, the peeler stuck in my skull.

"Even if they make me forget, I don't want to forgive you," I say. "I hope part of me still knows not to accept any more dinner invitations."

"You wouldn't be the only one missing pieces at our table. Sometimes, that's what it takes to join the family. Sometimes, it makes them want what we have more.”

I can't wipe my tears, but I can meet her eyes. “That's how a lot of terrible things work. But you *are* missing a piece, Zoe. I'm sorry it took meeting your family for me to finally see the hole you inherited. And what you're missing is so much more than what your mother is going to take from me.”

She smiles sadly. “I am missing something. I just didn't know until this year that it was you.”

“No person is going to replace what's missing, not for long.”

“I'm not a monster, Sierra.”

“You keep telling yourself that.”

“You won't remember this,” Zoe says, although she's not looking at me anymore. “You won't remember.”

“Sweetheart, she's going to need you more than ever.” Mother comes around my chair with another tray, this one carried instead of slid across the floor. She hands Zoe a fresh towel. “She needs to bite down on this.”

“Oh my God…” I attempt to climb out of the bindings again with increasing urgency that does nothing to improve the effectiveness of my efforts. The chain links connecting the cuffs to the metal arms and legs of the chair jangle more and more violently.

On the tray lays a standard hunting knife next to a bone saw. And on the stove, another cast-iron pan—or maybe the same one—warms on a flaming burner.

“Oh my God, no. No, no, *no*. Please don't do this. I'll eat anything you give me. I'll eat an eyeball. I'll eat a whole fucking brain, raw. Please don't do it. Please don't cut me! No!” I'm not even paying attention to what I'm saying anymore, just a string of pleas that fall on indifferent ears.

Mother's jaw is set, her gaze resolute. She is certain, as I have never been certain in my life, because she is Mother and has had time to carve that face into the mountain. Even though the lights cover us from every angle, she casts an encompassing shadow, making me dull and her painfully clear, filling my vision.

Mother rests a finger on my lips to shush me. I'm too scared for even stream of consciousness now. I've made headway on the cuff, but not enough. Not enough. Not in time.

"You cut short my feast by two courses, and you tried to run. I'll make it so that not only will you never be able to run again, you'll eat those feet you already stuffed into your mouth."

I scream as loudly as I can. Mother winces from the contained volume, especially without anything in the room to absorb it.

"You're going to continue to resist, rebel. That's understandable." Somehow, her warm, low, even tone cuts through my high-pitched frequency. "But Zoe's going to gag you with the towel now. It's not to stop you from expressing yourself so much as to keep you from biting off your tongue when we begin. This won't be as fast as the cleaver, unfortunately. It's an unfortunate angle, and we already established that you can't be trusted if we remove the cuffs. Zoe, please."

As I'm screaming, Zoe brings the towel around my face from behind. She stuffs the terrycloth thick into my conveniently open mouth, pushing back my tongue in the process and keeping me from being able to bite much at all.

"Just hang on," she whispers, her breath hot on my cheek. She holds me like a crazed horse with a bit. "If you feel yourself starting to faint, don't fight it. The pills should kick in soon. They'll help. Just hang on." As though she's my champion, rooting for me every second of my struggle, and not the struggle itself.

I want to be angry with her, but then Mother switches on the powered bone saw. It's shriller than a chainsaw or table saw, like an electric toothbrush, except this toothbrush is going to brush bone clean from bone, and it's got layers of muscle to go through before the foot is severed.

"It's best if I do this quickly, dear, although it won't feel like it to you."

Mother brings the bone saw to the shin, waiting just under skin. I fight the cuffs and pray adrenaline can tear thick leather, but neither God nor god hears, and the goddess has already stitched my fate.

She saws bone-deep pain then tears through fiber until the saw judders the metal leg, tossing shavings to the ground amid the horror show at my feet— of my foot. I scream my throat to shreds, and still my brain is not merciful. I have no words, no choice. The world is nothing but bright steel, too much glare, almost suffocating as I inhale the towel halfway down my throat. Zoe pulls it back out again. If I had anything left inside of me, I would curse her for it.

My jaw is locked into the terrycloth, however, so at Mother's nod, Zoe abandons me to run to the stove. She brings the pan to the flailing base of my stump after Mother cuts with the knife through what little she missed with the saw. Mother puts her weight on my leg to hold it down as Zoe cauterizes the stump, curdling blood, although I've lost enough to make my head turn while pain already drowns me.

I don't last through the sweet, metallic burning of flesh searching through the nubbly towel to my nostrils to tantalize, like anything else Mother cooks. I hope I die full.

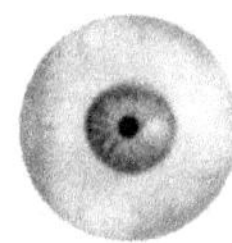

When I wake, I haven't enough space in my skull for despair. It spills out my nose and ungagged mouth, down my throat in bloody salt from a nosebleed, perhaps from holding my breath or bearing down. I no longer wail but weep, which sounds like things that women in sepia tones do with lace handkerchiefs, but I'm not screaming at the walls anymore. If anyone heard me, it's already too late. I feel what's not there.

They adjusted the cuffs to just above the knee, a little too tight—not enough to tourniquet, because cooked flesh seals me in. The bottoms of my legs, cross-sectioned halfway up my shins, are brown with iodine rather than blood. Bleach penetrates the mucosal coating with its chemical sting.

I wish I made a bigger impression, a bigger mess, but I am clean but for stains in my leggings, and the room has been tended like a hospital stay while I slept.

My feet, washed and rubbed with a roast blend, spin in

slow, dizzy circles in one of the rotisserie ovens.

"Drink this." I recognize Zoe's manicure. She holds a plastic cup of orange juice with a straw.

"You can't do this to me. You can't—"

But when Zoe pushes the straw between my chapped lips, I drink, desperately thirsty.

"The faster we finish here, the sooner we can get you found. The hospital will deal with the worst of it." She wipes off some of the blood from my nose. "I'll help you every step of the way after that. Lunch is almost finished. We have so much gravy left over from last night. Would you like to help us get through that, or would you rather digest your feet on their own?"

I stare at her without answering. I don't feel like myself. Everything about me is screaming, including what's changed on a molecular level in the rotisserie oven. Everything except my voice. The pills make the pain less important, distant, like chatter in the dormitory hallways while I'm trying to sleep, but I know it waits just on the other side of the door.

Zoe's changed, too. She's not a goddess's daughter anymore. Not the popular girl slumming it with the shy. Not the gorgeous amateur model.

She's just a girl.

"I'll warm up some gravy," Zoe says, although she seems disquieted by the way I stare at her, perhaps because it's not with hatred or fear, which she might know how to turn.

She returns with another plastic cup, this time of red wine, which I don't think is supposed to mix with my pills. I sip anyway. I don't see myself operating any heavy machinery.

The rotisserie oven beeps. My feet keep rotating.

Zoe arranges the gravy on the sliding tray with the wine. Then she retrieves my feet from the oven. My flesh is darker and tougher than chicken, but she's meticulous about removing every bit of edible meat from each little bone, including the toes. No nails on the plate. She keeps the discards on a separate tray.

"What do you do with the bones?" The voice from my throat is not mine. I sound like I've lost five rounds to bronchitis.

A smile lifts hopefully at her lips' corners now that I'm finally talking to her. "Bone broth and soup stock. Marrow butter from the bigger bones."

"You have an answer for everything."

"Hunting is nothing new, not even our prey. The principles stay the same from squirrel to sorority sister."

"I'd rather have squirrel."

"I'm sorry. We only have sole." Zoe arranges the meat around the gravy bowl. She tries a piece without the gravy, then raises her eyebrows with a hum, pleased.

She doesn't undo my bindings but instead sits next to me to feed me one foot, then the other—or maybe both at the same time. All cut up, I can't tell my left foot from my right; with the gravy, it's more like a stew and all ends up in the same place. I alternate between wanting to laugh and wanting to cry, but I'm incapable of both. It sits behind the same door as the pain.

She eats with me, and of me, and between the both of us, we polish the plate.

That people are eating leftover turkey and stuffing

sandwiches, shopping Black Friday deals in stores or online, watching movies all through their full-belly second holiday seems impossible. If Zoe were to drag me outside to scorched, smoking earth, with only the Samuels' house standing, green lawn and all, I would not be shocked. Anything other than apocalypse isn't fair.

I gulp the wine when she tips the plastic glass. I have the strangest craving for chocolate cherry cordial, the sweet blood clot on top, although I really couldn't eat another bite.

"This wasn't how I saw the feast ending," Zoe says, lowering her eyes. "I feel just sick about how pale you look. The sugar and the meat will help, but I know it must… I nearly screamed when you screamed, cried when you cried. I don't know how people do this."

She touches my face, then goes to the sink for a new washcloth to wipe the worst from around my nose and mouth until my face feels shrunken dry but clean, at least, while pain trickles into the empty room like new tide.

She shifts her hand so that it's her fingers touching my mouth again, not the washcloth, which she lets fall to the floor with a wet splat. I twitch, remembering my foot falling into its own splatter pool, but there's no use crying over spilled blood now. Nothing for a doctor to sew back on but bone. I chewed the muscle, fat, skin. I was delightful; after all, Mother cooked me.

Zoe drifts her fingertips down to my neck, to the neckline. She finds my nipple through the shirt and bralette, keeps her strokes light but not tentative, intent as she watches the nipple stiffen through the fabric. Even someone emptied of a few pints can flush and tighten and spare a fingerful for arousal—purely physical, like the feeling of my toes flexing beneath the bindings. The iodine might as well be honey for fire ants, but I can't scratch and I probably shouldn't. My breath hitches.

Zoe spreads her hand to cover my breast. "You're becoming part of me. You're inside of me."

She slides the tray away, then her chair, makes her own shadow over me, although she isn't the same intimidating figure as Mother. She still plays with my breast, but she trails her other hand down my thigh to the knee, her hair a wild tousle as she inspects the abrupt end. I swallow against the trapdoor of my throat.

"I'll be there when you get back. I won't leave you alone." She bothers the cells of me still stifled-screaming, then slides her hand back up my thigh to under the hem of my shirt. "Don't leave me, Sierra."

When she kisses me, tasting my meat and the wine on my tongue, I don't bite. Then she slips her legs under the chair arms and straddles my thighs. Despite the pressure on sensitive flesh, I don't whimper, except when I respond to a bolder caress.

I can wish forever that things were different, but that won't make me regurgitate feet whole from my stomach, and it won't make the taste of us any less laced innocent.

So close to me, she can't see how I close my palm over the fork handle and saw again at the binding, but when I'm loud and she's loud, we cover the scratch of it, distracted instead by the chair groans and the resonance of our little sounds against all the hard surfaces. Soon, they're both sincere, the kisses and the sawing. I want us under covers on a cheap, squeaking bed, naked and warm, laughing where no one can hear us, legs tangled in the sheets. I want birthdays and exploration. I want her hair spun around my fingers as she shades me from the sun and I peer through her glasses at pale eyes. I want her, but the way we should have been. And maybe if they make me forget, we can be that way again. Nothing about our legs wound in sheets requires my feet.

But if I forget and she infiltrates the strange muscle of my heart, she'll bring me back here again.

Maybe by that time, if she introduces me Mother's way, I'll cheer a tube down some poor man's throat, filling his stomach with extra brown gravy when he asks if Mother has any white.

A little serotonin is supposed to help with pain. I might have already thought that before; it rings like a déjà vu echo. But I can't remember, can't focus on anything other than what I desire to be true and the frantic sawing of the leather.

Maybe she thinks I'm just struggling to hold her. She reaches back to the cuff over my right wrist and, without looking, frantically undoes the buckle. I can't believe it at first—even more unbelievable than everything else. The fork hits the metal arm with a clank that Zoe must dismiss as one of the links.

I don't let myself hesitate, although my already fluttering heart seems to jerk in my chest like a fist from behind. I think of Zoe in the courtyard, with a chocolate fudge bar and a university t-shirt, enjoying low evening light, the first time the sun spun her to gold…and I stab the fork straight into her neck.

She shakes in a ripple, her mouth open in my hair. She falls back on my thighs and fumbles at the fork.

I jerk and twist, hard. If it were the cheap cutlery of the cafeteria, perhaps I would do more damage to the metal than Zoe's delicate balance of artery and vein, but Mother's utensils are of sturdy stock. When I finally yank out the steel plug, her neck vents like a faucet. My hand is a red glove, but I have such a hold on the fork that the handle slips only from sweat.

I'm more of a mess than before, and so is she. She tries to speak, but she bleeds out too quickly and with too much surprise for words. The betrayal in her beautiful eyes doesn't begin to match what churns in my cramping abdomen. As she collapses back, her legs slip from under chair arms. She falls, undignified, onto her back in the new blood pool, spreading.

I don't let go of the fork, but I fumble with the binding on my left wrist. More delicately, I undo the buckles on my legs, hissing in and out every time I jostle the flesh left under my knee.

When the bindings fall away, swinging on the arms or clinking down to the base of the bolted chair, I breathe. I breathe.

But I can't just breathe. Mother may be giving her daughter time, but that time isn't forever. Fortunately, the fact Mother doesn't thunder in means there's no camera aimed at me, or at least that she's giving her daughter more privacy than the feast provided.

Still holding the fork, I gingerly shift onto my knees on the hard seat. I can't depend on the pills to carry me through while using the stumps, so I lean on the integrity of my knees, which still requires me to flex muscles seared at their ends.

I climb down into the pool of Zoe's blood and leave a snail trail of her as I pull myself forward on elbows and hands, neither of which are ideal, but I don't have a choice. Removing my feet was the penalty for trying to run. I won't survive the day or night or whatever it is if Mother walks in on her beloved daughter dead.

I veer off course for the pegboard. I would have to stand on my stumps to reach even the lowest of implements on the board, but Mother's tray of bone saw and knife, on the counter to dry after being cleaned, is more manageable, and only one of the tools isn't confined by a power cord.

I'm almost at the short set of stairs when Mother unlocks and opens the door, holding a little leather medical bag like a clutch.

She sees me before the red, but when that catches her eye, I watch it fill her vision, as though it will pour like wine into the clear glass of her irises. A clatter and smear with every wriggle, I draw her attention back to me. With it comes the retraction of lips from teeth, shifting her from Mother to monster in less than a minute, but perhaps that's a matter of perspective as I crawl up toward her.

She shuts the door but doesn't lock it by the time I reach her. She tries to kick my face. I slash at her ankle just above her shoe, push myself up to slash at her shins like she cut at me with a saw, but I realize quickly that I hit the same bone without the same power behind it. She stomps on the hand I use to keep myself upright, crunching my fingers like sunflower seeds and sending me reeling, unbalanced. My head almost hits the bottom stair.

Mother tries now to flood me with pain by resurrecting the worst of the damage she inflicted, still singing in every serpentine strain of my body, but panic pairs with the opioid to quell it without more direct pain, and Mother can't reach my stumps fast enough. Instead, in trying, she gives me access to the fleshy part of her leg, the vulnerable tendon behind her foot.

I slash again, and this time I do more than surface damage. The butcher knife slices far better than the carving knife. I don't quite cut the Achilles completely, but I nick it. Her knee buckles when the rest of the leg gives out. That gives the arc of my swing more to aim for.

She screams, kicks, screams, and I scream, slash, scream. She's much louder than me because her throat isn't a woodchipper lined with splinters and terrycloth lint, but if anyone in the house hears her, they'll assume she's me. Who else would be screaming?

"You fucking bitch!" Mother fumbles with the bag's zipper, jerks it open to a collection of syringes and vials. Precise work when being attacked by ninety percent of a girl soaked in a daughter's blood.

I use the knife in her thigh to pull me closer, which also puts her in reach of my hair, but I rock up as high as I can and stab the knife into her belly with all the weight and strength I have left.

It gives like nothing on her leg, which is dense muscle to bone. Fat and a layer of muscle yield to the squishy soft interior. Once inside, as with Zoe, I cut, twist, then yank back out to let the insides flow. I'm hit with blood but also the powerful odor of shit from an intestine still full from feasting. Blood spills; the rest stays more or less in place.

"You ungrateful—"

I slash again, this time at her mouth, clefting both lips and catching her tongue.

Mother splutters and bubbles, covers her mouth with both hands in disbelief, like Zoe before her. Their resemblance in blood intensifies.

If Mother let me, I would show her more mercy than she showed me, but the only reason why I could do that for Zoe was the element of surprise. Mother can't believe, but surprise is out of the question, so her death is slower.

"George... George..." She tries to scream again, but the abdominal wound is a gut punch.

I don't need to wait until she dies, just until she's quiet. Then I climb, dragging new and newer blood up the stairs with me, knife clinking every time I slam my hand down. The door is unlocked. I don't have a key to lock it behind me. I have to risk Mother rallying.

At the door to the back room, I pause, panting, exhausted. Cold sweat like late autumn dew coats my face and neck and all under my shirt—or maybe that's blood.

I don't know what company they're hosting. Even if everyone's gone home, that's still a father and two daughters who could walk in on me, and I can barely crawl. I can't trust anyone in their neighborhood any more than I could when I was fully ambulatory, and people might still be travelling for the holidays. In the meantime, I could get or already have an infection. I could go into shock. I could disturb the burnt flesh enough to trigger more blood flow than seepage. I could die before I reach the front door.

Knife hand forward, glass-cut hand forward, knee crawl, knee crawl. I shuffle along the wall and hope that staying out of the way—if not out of view—keeps anyone from noticing the blood in my wake.

Two long lengths of live-edge table and benches, empty. I need to stop when I reach the foot of the table. I slump on the floor, slick forehead on my crossed arms. The wine and the pills conspire to pitch me forward even while I'm almost flat, but I force myself back to hands and knees, from hardwood to tile.

The dessert table is gone. What desserts people left are now in place of the wine bottles. I consider taking my cookies as a consolation prize and fuck you to the hosts who couldn't appreciate them. In the end, it's the loud packaging that dissuades me. I check the hutch's lower cabinets for my purse, but I can't find it anywhere.

"Damn it." I pound my fists on the floor, then choke on my own breath listening if anyone heard.

I creep forward again, the most ungainly, loud, filthy trespasser on the planet—but to be fair, I was invited.

Layla enters the kitchen and opens the fridge.

I freeze, or try to. I slip on the tile and slide forward. I stifle my gasp and brief loss of breath in my arm, but the only reason Layla doesn't spin around is because she's listening to something on her phone, earbuds visible through her loose hair.

She stands in front of the fridge. Its cool air sweeps me shivering. Finally, she pulls out a bottled juice blend, closes the fridge door, and leaves. I'm sure she'll see me, but she doesn't hesitate.

I crawl into the kitchen, trying to tell if anyone else is coming from either direction. Nothing, although I'm still panting like I've sprinted around the entire college campus five times. Not something I'll be doing any time soon.

I pull myself out of the kitchen. My arms are shaking, nausea pitches my guts, vertigo rocks my world, and I'm cold in all the wrong ways, except the ends of my legs, which are awakening from the initial pharmaceutical suppression and threatening to be worse than what put me under last time, because this time it'll be two-fold.

"Hey."

Halfway along the wood panels lining the stairs, I freeze again, my lungs hole-ridden bellows. Panic shallows the panting further, to dizzying effect that almost commits me unconscious again.

Layla sits fifth step up, her face pressed against the spindles. She's not wearing earbuds anymore.

I wait for her to call for Mother, for Father, for Zoe, but she just rests her head against the polished wood, looking as tired as I am, if cleaner. She has the same pale eyes that run in her family. The whites are red, but not in a way that suggests she's been crying—more like they dry out, perhaps from lack of sleep.

Layla reaches through the spindles. My purse dangles from her arm. "I charged your phone."

I take the purse, although blood loss and surprise stun my tongue. I hook the strap around me so I won't have to carry it and the knife.

"Leave a mark somewhere where they can't find it to wash it away. Prove you were here." Layla stands on the stairs, then walks around me and into the kitchen. "Father!"

I panic, crawling faster toward the front door.

But she continues, more distant and muffled by the walls between us as she heads toward the main suite. "Can I talk to you?"

"Back here, sweetie!" Father calls back, almost inaudible.

She's giving me time to escape. She doesn't know I've killed her sister and possibly Mother, but I'm covered with blood clearly not my own, since mine would mostly be below the knees. I don't know if either of their deaths would change things for her, but I can't afford to wait around to find out. I'm not going to get another chance. I just have to hope their sister Helena is occupied elsewhere.

Galvanized by her help, by the improved odds, I shuffle across the foyer rug. At the front door, I look behind me at the obvious trail, although it's thinning and browning as the blood dries. I suppress a whine as I reach for the bottom of my right leg and gather blood on two fingers. A side table crouches next to the door in the entryway, adorned with a porcelain tea set and pewter teapot. I put my blood inside both the porcelain and pewter teapots. In case climbing up the sideboard left spots, I also slip my fingers underneath and smear more there. I don't know if it's enough, but I can't afford to deviate too much from my path, difficult as it is just to go from point A to point B.

By the time I reach the front door again, I'm whimpering from the pressure that extends from my knees and down my legs as I try to keep my stumps off the ground. I lean against the door to turn the deadbolt.

I strain to hear anything at all: Helena upstairs, Layla and Father in the back. Nothing, and if Father saw the blood, I would hope he'd exclaim loudly enough for me to hear or that Layla would make some effort to warn me.

When I open the door, the cold winter night buffets me like needles without my coat, but I grit my teeth, whining high in my nose as I crawl out, bracing myself on the handle. Then I pull the door closed behind me, doing my best to keep from shutting the door too loudly.

Tears spill over the unholy font of hope that I'll get out and certainty that they'll catch me, hope that I'll survive and certainty that I'll never really escape. Saliva catches on my lips and chin, mucus drips from my nose, and saltwater dries on my cheeks in the frigid wind, but I climb out of range of the front porch light and into darkness where it's harder to follow my tracks.

I crawl onto the lawn, fighting my impulse to scream, scream for help where people are more likely to hear me, because hearing me doesn't mean they'll help. I can't scream, because Father will hear that and drag me back in. Then no one will save me, no matter how loud I am. But I can't keep doing this, crawling with increasing agony in my legs all the way out the neighborhood like I'd planned when I tried to run.

I wriggle like a caterpillar across the brittle brown grass, around limestone-edged landscaping, and into the neighbor's yard. I crawl over mulch that feels like a thousand splinters on my exposed legs, but at least they have bushes.

My purse zipper seems too loud. For a moment, I think Layla played her own game and kept my phone to give me hope only to rip it away, but it's behind my wallet, dark because it's still off.

When I turn it on, it's a hundred percent charged, but it still takes forever to load. I leave smears of blood on the screen where I enter the unlock code, then dial *9-1-1*.

"9-1-1. Where is your emergency?"

It's on speaker. I can't afford for anyone to hear the voice on the other end, so the volume is low, but after using my arms more than my legs to crawl, to climb, to fight, to kill, I don't have the energy anymore to hold the phone up to my ear.

"My name is Sierra." I lean back on the brick wall of the neighbor's house, shivering from cold on cold sweat but also shaking from other things. The phone glow leaves its own trail of light in my hands like fireflies. "You're on speaker, so don't talk. I've been held captive by my roommate's family. I don't know the address. Their last name is Samuels. Mother's name is Marcie. Father's name is George. My roommate drove us here. This family… Don't make the mistake of thinking they're crazy. They're sadists and cannibals and terribly, terribly sane. They made a guy eat his hand and a woman eat her own cheeks for Thanksgiving dinner. They made us eat people. When a woman wouldn't, they forced her to eat her vomit. They made me eat my own feet after I tried to escape. I know this sounds like a prank, but it's not. I'm not losing much blood anymore, but I'm cold and I'm sweating and I'm in pain and I can't run. I'm hiding in the bushes next door. I don't want them to find me. Please send help. Please. Fucking please, send someone to stop them. They have leftovers. They have bones. I have blood on me. I had to fight back. I had to do it. I had to…"

The crying becomes less about hope and relief and despair and more about pale white-blue eyes empty in a scarlet pool.

"Please help me. I don't want them to find me. Please don't let them find me."

"Ma'am," intones the calm voice on the other end, "I'm sending police and paramedics to the GPS location of your cell."

"I'm next door" is all I can manage through the thick wetness gumming my mouth.

"Are you to the right or left?"

"I crawled to the right. God, don't let me die. Don't let them know."

"Police are five minutes out, fire and paramedics ten minutes out. They're going in lights but no sirens."

"Don't hurt Layla," I mutter. Vision swims and the world tilts like too much vodka.

"Is Layla your roommate?"

"My roommate is dead. I killed her because she fed me my feet."

The dispatcher is quiet for a long time, or maybe I drift off. "Ma'am, are there children in the house?"

"I don't know. Layla's older. Their other older sister might still be upstairs, too."

I drift off again.

The next thing I know are lights, blue and red, so damn patriotic. No sirens, as promised. I don't understand why they don't swarm the house. They slam their doors but mill on the sidewalk, speaking into their shoulders.

"Sierra, are you still there? Can you hear me? Are you awake?"

"I'm here." I don't sound here. I sound a few feet in front of me. Shivering adds a tremulous vibrato into my reply.

"Are the police where you can see them? Are they in front of the right house?"

"Yes. I can see them. They're in front of the Samuels' house. The back room is where Zoe and Mother are, where they kept me. They keep a plastic container of bones. Leftovers in their fridge and freezer. I put my blood in their teapots. Please believe me. Even if they cleaned all my blood and took away the rug from the front, please believe me. Please believe me."

An officer hears me, tilts his head to follow my voice. My first impulse is to stay hidden until the Samuels family is caught and I know that this isn't all in my head. Maybe the only leftovers in the fridge and freezer are turkey and ham. Maybe the back room is a sunroom that leads to the backyard. Maybe I didn't kill anyone and Zoe's streaming shows on her tablet in her room upstairs. Maybe I still have my feet.

I still want to hide, but I can't crawl anymore.

"Oh my God."

My face screws up as though trying to spiral inward, hide itself. I cry again, more sound than salt, because I feel dry as bone and cured meat. The officer's reaction is all I need to know.

"Dispatch, we found her." The officer approaches me in a crouch, shadow silhouetted against flashing red and blue. I don't feel safe, and he holds up his hands to calm me. "I'm going to carry you out. Paramedics are almost here."

"Front door is open," I manage, but I don't let go of my phone and I don't stop leaning away from him. He relays the information into his radio. "They weren't going to kill me, but they were never really going to let me go. You have to believe me."

"I believe you. I believe you."

But it's just something you say to a hysterical child, and why not? I am a hysterical child, and I'm freezing and shocked and exhausted and drugged and unable to fight when the officer tucks his arms behind me and under my knees, although I strangle new screams at the pull on the stumps after sitting here all this time.

"My God," he mutters. "Where are the goddamn paramedics?"

"It's not my blood." I hold up the knife, which is stuck to my hand with clots.

"It's okay, sweetie. Carpenter, get a bag for the knife."

"They gave me pills and wine and vodka. I threw up the vodka. I didn't throw up people. Please believe me."

As my officer requests backup over his radio, other officers rush the front door, unlocked, which means Layla kept Father occupied. I close my eyes and pray to I don't know who—*the goddess is dead*—that none of it happened, that they dosed us with psilocybin in the saltless soup at the feast's beginning, that

I've only ruined an unconventional family's nice post-Thanksgiving evening.

They bring Father out in handcuffs. He sees me still in the officer's arms. His brown eyes are haunted white on the edges, like Leslie's.

"Oh God, what is this place?" says someone on the radio.

"They keep some of us alive," I say to the officer and to the dispatcher still on the bright phone screen. "You'll find Leslie without a hand and Tawna with her face and part of her tongue missing. They won't remember. Gloria might have food poisoning. We're what happens when we don't do what we're told. We have to eat and drink everything. Those are the rules. We have to finish the feast."

"We'll look into it. Sergeant, you hearing this?" my officer says. "She's really out of it, but I don't necessarily think she's delirious."

"Copy. This place is FUBAR."

Layla comes out with her hands behind her back, too, as the fire engine and EMS pull onto the street, but she doesn't have the pinched tension of Father; her forehead is ironed perfectly smooth. She meets my dead eyes with hers. She nods to me, like we're at the end of the same race she already accepted she would lose.

"We're going to need another bus," someone else says over the radio. "Two females, DOA. Three more bodies and parts frozen in the iceboxes. It's a fucking slaughterhouse in here."

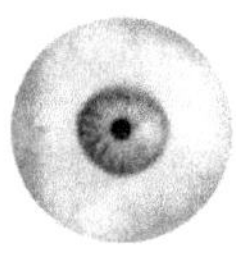

Not a slaughterhouse. A catering company.

A lot comes out over the next few weeks, information that expands from local news to state-wide to national. I'm too disconnected to care that I go viral, although at one point Mom and Dad have to screen and vet all my communication and mail to eliminate the creeps and keep gifted plants from smothering me with oxygen.

The Samuelses and their extended family and associates are gradually arrested or given deals. Their web of specialized underground menus solves several missing persons cases as well as assaults like mine, where the most unusual pieces are missing in individuals found drugged and wandering.

The money dries up; the empire crumbles. People talk. But not to me. I refuse interviews with anyone without a gold badge or subpoena. Mom and Dad field the rest with a form reply or no comment.

I won't eat. While my parents are in the cafeteria, the nurse sets up my feeding tube. She asks me what people taste like. I don't answer, because it's temperature and seasoning that determines flavor more than the meat.

I'm handcuffed to my hospital bed until I'm not. I'm kept sedated until I'm not. I answer questions more than a dozen times, or maybe only eight, because I might answer some no one asks when no one is there, or I think I answer but the detective repeats the question because I haven't.

I see Layla in the part of the hospital where we're kept as soon as they manage to quell the infection from the burns, which requires some additional removal of my legs, almost up to the knees. Turns out cauterization is not the answer to amputation, not that Mother cared about anything but her cooking. I told my surgeons that a few more inches off make no difference to me, and I laughed because it's funny.

When I come back to the university in the fall to start over, I see Layla some more. We don't talk, at least to each other. I don't ask if she hates me, and she doesn't ask if I hate her.

They say I can eventually try prostheses, but I have more physical and psychological therapy to go through before we get to that point. In the meantime, I don't mind the wheelchair, even having to roll a steep uphill to classes and having to brake all the way back down, or waiting for elevators, for accessible bathroom stalls. I'm not angry about that, although it still seems unreal, like someone took an eraser and smudged me beneath my knees, and sometimes the whole emptiness itches like fire ants in honey still.

They make me look in a mirror when that happens. It helps, but the person in the mirror looks like someone's incomplete sketch, and not just what's below my knees.

What I really don't like is the smells.

Not mine. I have a bench in the suite bathroom, and bars. My arms are stronger than they used to be.

I don't like when people cook in the dorm kitchen. I don't like the cafeteria. I don't like the food people bring into classrooms, their deafening chewing, obscene swallowing.

Layla and I are both treated for eating disorders; the only

thing we can keep down is juice mixes. Orange mango is my new communion. I have a juicer and a blender. I render food unrecognizable and with minimal smell in their cup. The nutritionists recommend a protein powder to add to them at least once a day. I put the straw at the back of my mouth so I barely have to taste.

At my insistence, my new roommate is vegan.

THE END?

Not if you want to dive into more of Crystal Lake Publishing's Tales from the Darkest Depths!

Check out our amazing website and online store or download our latest catalog here: https://geni.us/CLPCatalog.

We always have great new projects and content on the website to dive into, as well as a newsletter, behind the scenes options, social media platforms, our own dark fiction shared-world series and our very own webstore. Our webstore even has categories specifically for KU books, non-fiction, anthologies, and of course more novels and novellas.

AUTHOR BIOGRAPHY

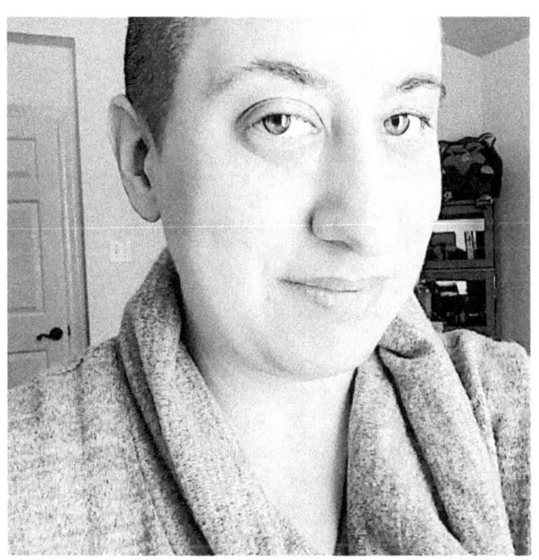

A mass of tentacles and rose vines masquerading as a person, Amanda M. Blake is the author of such horror titles as *Deep Down* and *Out of Curiosity and Hunger*, dark poetry collection *Dead Ends*, and the Thorns fairy tale mash-up series. For more, visit amandamblake.com.

Readers…

Thank you for reading *Question Not My Salt*. We hope you enjoyed this novel. If you have a moment, please review *Question Not My Salt* at the store where you bought it.

Help other readers by telling them why you enjoyed this book. No need to write an in-depth discussion. Even a single sentence will be greatly appreciated. Reviews go a long way to helping a book sell, and is great for an author's career. It'll also help us to continue publishing quality books.

Thank you again for taking the time to journey with Crystal Lake's Torrid Waters.

You will find links to all our social media platforms on our Linktree page: https://linktr.ee/CrystalLakePublishing.

MISSION STATEMENT

Since its founding in August 2012, Crystal Lake Publishing has quickly become one of the world's leading publishers of Dark Fiction and Horror books. In 2023, Crystal Lake Publishing formed a part of Crystal Lake Entertainment, joining several other divisions, including Torrid Waters, Crystal Lake Comics, and many more.

While we strive to present only the highest quality fiction and entertainment, we also endeavour to support authors along their writing journey. We offer our time and experience in non-fiction projects, as well as author mentoring and services, at competitive prices.

With several Bram Stoker Award wins and many other wins and nominations (including the HWA's Specialty Press Award), Crystal Lake puts integrity, honor, and respect at the forefront of our publishing operations.

We strive for each book and outreach program we spearhead to not only entertain and touch or comment on issues that affect our readers, but also to strengthen and support the Dark Fiction field and its authors.

Not only do we find and publish authors we believe are destined for greatness, but we strive to work with men and women who endeavour to be decent human beings who care more for others than themselves, while still being hard-working, driven, and passionate artists and storytellers.

Crystal Lake is and will always be a beacon of what passion and dedication, combined with overwhelming teamwork and respect, can accomplish. We endeavour to know each and every one of our readers, while building personal relationships with our authors, reviewers, bloggers, podcasters, bookstores, and libraries.

This is what we believe in. What we stand for. This will be our legacy.

Welcome to Crystal Lake Entertainment

THANK YOU FOR PURCHASING THIS BOOK